Duchess of Destiny

An Allingham Regency Classic

Merryn Allingham

DUCHESS OF DESTINY

This novel is entirely a work of fiction. The names, characters and incidents portrayed in it are the work of the author's imagination. Any resemblance to actual persons, living or dead, events or localities is entirely coincidental.

First published in Great Britain 2017 by The Verrall Press

Cover art: Berni Stevens Book Cover Design
ISBN: 978-1-9997824-1-2
Copyright © Merryn Allingham
Merryn Allingham asserts the moral right to be identified as the author of this work.

Chapter One

'Hurry up, or the milk will have curdled!'

A titter of laughter rippled through the company. The tall figure of Gabriel Claremont, Duke of Amersham, Earl of Rycroft, Baron Everard, draped itself negligently against the warm stone of the building. His hands were thrust deep into his pockets as he surveyed the motley band of companions who had walked with him to the dairy. A pair of intensely blue eyes tempered an otherwise saturnine expression.

Elinor felt a poke in her ribs, then Martha handed her a tray laden with glasses of frothing milk. Scrambling up the steps of the creamery, she almost cannoned into the duke.

'Less haste, girl, or there will be no milk left to drink.'

There was another titter. Half a dozen men and women had arranged themselves at intervals around the little iron-work tables scattered along the terrace. This was the latest *ton* fad, Martha had told her, to drink milk straight from the cow.

'Your Grace.' Elinor curtsied briefly and handed him a glass.

For a moment he towered over her, one of the few

men she'd encountered tall enough to do so. Dressed in riding-breeches and top boots with a Belcher handkerchief loosely knotted about his neck, he was unlikely to pose a challenge to Brummell, but though he was perfunctorily dressed, his broad chest exuded an uncomfortable male strength.

She snatched a quick glance at his face and a lead weight nudged a path to her heart. It couldn't be him. He was too young. Far too young to have known her mother. He seemed strangely familiar, though, and she looked again. Yes... she was certain he was the man who last evening had sent her headlong into a ditch. His air of casual disdain spoke an imperviousness to dairymaids and travellers alike. She had been forced to gather her skirts and leap for her life, catching only a flash of an upright figure, dark hair flying, before the racing curricle with its gilded crest was gone in a haze of dust.

'So what happened to Letty?' A man a few paces away sneered, his face weary with dissipation.

She met his look. His thin lips appeared to have been reddened, and was that rouge he wore on his cheeks? 'I don't know, sir,' she forced herself to say.

'Don't try to gammon me, girl! Servants know everything.'

He was a truly horrible man and she would have liked to throw the milk in his face. How on earth had she come to be in this situation? When she'd made her dawn escape from Bath, she'd realised that she was burning her boats. But this!

'Don't you talk?' It was another of His Grace's friends, a

wispy young man wearing the tightest coat Elinor had ever seen. 'Pretty high and mighty for a dairymaid, eh, Gabe?'

The duke had said nothing seeming not hear his companions, but she had felt him studying her intently. Now he turned to her.

'What is your name?'

'Nell Milford, Your Grace.'

'Nell. Short for Helen or Elinor or perhaps Margaret?'

'Elinor, sir.'

She had hoped no one would ask that question since she'd deliberately chosen Nell as a far more likely servant's name. When yesterday she had rounded that final bend in the road and seen the formidable gates of Amersham guarded by soldiers, she'd been suffused with panic. This couldn't be Amersham Hall – she must have taken the wrong road out of Steyning. She had walked through a quiet and green landscape, the hedgerows filled with the sweet scent of late May, but now with dusk falling she found herself stranded – outside a strange mansion in a strange locality, a lone woman, shabby and unkempt from two days' travelling. She would have been laughed out of sight if she were to ask for charity and a bed for the night. The older guard's question had been a lifebelt saving her from drowning. Was she the new dairymaid? Just pretend, she'd told herself, just pretend. 'Yes,' she'd said, and her voice had rung steady. 'I'm the new dairymaid, Elinor... Nell Milford.'

'Elinor,' the duke was musing now, 'an elegant name.'

'Elegant figure too,' guffawed a high-complexioned man sitting nearby.

'I prefer Letty's, don't you know.' It was the tight coat. 'A body you could get hold of.'

'And did, Hayward, as I recall – frequently.' This from the florid man. 'Too frequently by all accounts. It's no wonder she had to leave.'

'Don't be sad, Nell,' the man addressed as Hayward coaxed. 'You may not be such a plump pigeon, but I'm sure you have other attributes. She's mighty pretty, ain't she, Gabe?'

The duke ignored him and continued to lounge against the dairy wall, an expression of distaste on his face. His gaze wandered from her to the glass of milk he held and back again, and she watched his hesitation with inner amusement.

He put the glass down after only one sip and roused himself to say, 'Take no notice of my friends, Nell. They have yet to learn their manners.'

'I don't, Your Grace.' She thought of the locket secreted in her dress and her resolve stiffened. 'Courtesy does not come naturally to all.'

'Listen to that – and from a servant.' The rouged man had risen from his chair as though he would come towards her. She had to quell an overpowering urge to flee.

'Off with her head, eh, Weatherby?' someone quipped.

The duke seemed to have disappeared into his own thoughts once more, oblivious of his companions' pleasantries. They deserved each other, she decided. He might be good looking in a careless fashion, and no doubt he was extremely wealthy, but he was as haughty and ill-mannered as they. Her leap into the ditch yesterday had been a foretaste of what was to come. She should have kept walking past those gates.

Or should she? She had nowhere else she could go, that was the stark truth. She had not made a mistake. There was no other Amersham Hall in the district and this grand house was indeed the one she sought. For now at least she had employment, a roof over her head, and food in her stomach. But the notion that there could be any possible connection between her, this enormous property, and the heedless pleasure seeker standing so close, was nonsensical. As she had always suspected, Grainne had been delirious, her words provoked by fever.

'Good morning, Gabriel.'

A new voice had entered the fray. A neatly attired gentleman, no older than the duke himself and with a passing resemblance to him, was strolling towards the creamery from the opposite direction. His demeanour was one of a modest man and he had a pleasant but unremarkable face. The duke did not seem particularly pleased to see the new arrival and made no attempt to greet him beyond a brief nod in his direction.

The man ignored the rest of the group and instead turned to Elinor. 'I am the duke's cousin, Roland Frant. I live close by at the Dower House. You must be the new dairymaid.'

She nodded her agreement.

'And this is your first morning?'

'It is, sir.'

He looked closely at her face. 'I hope that you will be happy here.'

'I'm sure I will, Mr Frant.' Her voice did not hold conviction.

'Might I ask for a glass of milk, too?' He gestured to the table where half-empty tumblers were scattered in disarray.

'I will fetch it, sir.'

Escape at last. She wondered if Roland Frant had seen her agitation and deliberately allowed her to disappear.

'Spoiling the fun, Frant?' the thin-faced man jeered. Roland merely smiled complacently.

'Show's over, folks.' Hayward jumped to his feet, seeming keen to be gone now that the entertainment was at an end.

'Why do you have such a killjoy for a cousin, Gabe?' the thin-faced man asked.

Gabriel Claremont did not answer. Instead he said, 'I need to check on the stables. Emperor looked as though he was throwing a fever last night and I want him ready for the races on Friday.'

～

Gabriel could not be sure which warranted his greatest contempt, Roland's ingratiating airs or the boorishness of his friends. The word 'friends' was a misnomer; he had no friends, just people who gravitated towards his power and wealth and helped him fill the endless hours. When he'd first returned to England, he had welcomed any company. Jonathan was dead and he was distraught. He must take his brother's rightful place, play the imposter, or so it felt. No wonder he had surrounded himself with a wall of mindless chatter and pointless action. It had insulated him from reality since he could not face the world undisguised.

Life became one long dream through which he blundered, never quite hearing the voices or feeling the handshakes, never quite present. Day after day, month after month, time had blurred and been filled with an indeterminate noise that kept the void at bay. The ramshackle crowd he entertained had been that noise, but they were not his friends. They never would be. Jonathan had been his only friend and he was dead.

Something about the girl had reminded him of his brother, not that he needed any reminder, for the memory never left him. He wasn't certain what it was about her. Not her colouring for sure; that pale skin and those green eyes were striking in the extreme. Maybe it was the shape of her face or her tall, slender figure or just her expression – resolute and undaunted. It was an absurd connection to make, but he'd been so caught up in the fantasy that he'd hardly registered what his companions were about. He should have realised what was happening and stepped in to protect her. Instead it had been left to Roland to stop the spiteful bantering. Roland, the tell-tale of their childhood, the sly manipulator of their adult years.

The truth was that he lived too much in the past. But this morning, as he'd watched her and noticed her every movement, past and present had fused together. She was certainly an unusual dairymaid. Her face was too refined and her voice too cultivated, but cultivated or not she must be Letty's replacement. She was as slim as Letty had been an armful. Slim and fashioned grey. Only the white close-buttoned bodice relieved the Quaker hues and that had been starched into subjection.

She had waited while he drank the wretched milk, eyes downcast and hands clasped demurely in front of her. He'd been silently cursing this latest craze of *ton* society and grimacing in distaste when the girl's hands had most definitely twitched. Curiously he'd allowed his glance to travel upwards. She was looking directly at him, her eyes the shade of misty lake water, but seemingly lit by an inner delight. She had been laughing at him! Her wide mouth, far too wide, had trembled slightly as though in danger of breaking into irrepressible laughter at any moment. And though he'd stared back haughtily enough, he'd been fascinated. Seeing his look she had lowered her eyes once more and stilled the vagrant hands. An unusual dairymaid indeed! For the first time in years, he felt curiosity stir.

Chapter Two

The midday meal was a snatched event and Elinor had barely finished her last mouthful when there was a general commotion in the room and the sound of a hundred chairs being scraped back and a hundred pairs of feet shuffling on flagstones. Alongside her fellows, she rose from her seat before she realised the cause of the flurry. The duke was here in the servants' hall! A suppressed excitement thrummed around the vast space; a visit from the master of Amersham was something quite out of the ordinary.

The duke waited for silence to fall before he spoke, all the while looking blankly into the distance. 'My apologies for interrupting your meal,' he began in a voice devoid of expression, 'but I will not keep you long. There are few occasions when I can speak to you all and I believe that sometimes it is important to do so.'

He paused and cleared his throat. He seemed almost nervous, she thought, but that was ridiculous.

'We have several servants amongst us who have lately come to Amersham,' he began again.

The butler was looking perplexed and one or two of the

maids began to whisper behind their hands. The duke was no longer gazing into the distance but straight at Elinor, his blue eyes unfathomable. Surely he could not be talking to her.

'Several new people have come among us,' the duke repeated awkwardly. 'I trust that those of you who are well-established here will do all you can to make them welcome.'

Mr Jarvis was looking even more perplexed since it was his duty as butler to ensure the smooth running of the household, and here was his master seeming to take on that responsibility himself. There was another long silence while feet began to fidget and a few fingers to tap the table.

'I have no more to say,' the duke finished abruptly, 'other than to wish you well in your work. Please return to your meal.'

In an instant he had disappeared through the doorway and the room erupted into a buzz of speculation. It needed Mr Jarvis to clap his hands very loudly before the babble subsided. Nobody, it seemed, had any idea what to make of their master's unusual visit. Elinor had her suspicions – the duke had looked at *her*. She was sure that he had been speaking directly to her. Did he regret the unpleasantness she'd suffered this morning and wish to make some kind of apology? The only kind he could make without involving his horrible friends? An apology hardly fitted the man she'd met, for she had felt him to be proud and indifferent. It was a puzzle certainly, but now was not the time to solve it. She was already late for Martha and the dairy.

Last night she had noticed little of her surroundings,

other than the dark shape of the building hunched over a landscape which appeared to stretch for miles since she had been intent on concocting a believable history for herself before she reached the servants' quarters. And this morning she had been too tired to open her eyes, but now as she walked back to the creamery she could see the house was immense. The central mass resembled nothing less than a crenellated fortress with two equally forbidding wings marching right and left. The creamery lay at the end of the furthest wing and along a pathway of grey slabs. It was an attractive building. A row of double windows washed sunlight through its large, airy space and everywhere a sense of order prevailed, from the freshly washed cream and blue tiled walls to the storage tables dotted with jugs and cups of various sizes to the long shelf of white-veined marble lying bare and ready for butter-making.

'About time, too!'

Martha, perspiring and red-faced, was already labouring at one of the two huge cylindrical butter churns that sat in the middle of the open space. She was well into middle age, her face and body strongly marked by years of heavy work. Elinor felt scorched by the unfamiliar rudeness but she was a servant now, she reminded herself, and must learn to endure discourtesy.

'I'm sorry to have kept you waiting, Martha.'

The woman sniffed, evidently unimpressed by her new *protégée*. 'What did yer say yer name wuz again?'

'Nell, Nell Milford.'

'Well, Nell Milford, if yer to last longer than Letty, be 'ere on time. I needs to eat, too. Now you are 'ere, get going

13

on the turnin'. The Prince Regent brings fifty servants with 'im and all of 'em have to be fed.'

Elinor gaped. 'The Prince Regent is staying at Amersham Hall?'

'Often stays with His Grace. Don't stand there gawpin', girl – get goin'.' And she indicated the second churn standing close by.

That explained the soldiers. If the Prince Regent himself were staying, an armed guard would be thought necessary. It was another blow. Amersham Hall and its inhabitants were far from what she'd imagined and she had been a fool to come. But what had been the alternative? Without her mother's paintings to sell, an already meagre life had quickly descended into one of abject poverty. She had tried and failed to find work. Her singular education had left her unfit to be a governess and she was too well known in the town to become a servant. The ladies of Bath would never employ an obviously genteel girl, no matter how poor, since it was too sharp a reminder of the fragile border between success and failure.

At first it had been easy to dismiss her mother's dying words as delirium, but then as her situation had grown more and more desperate, they had returned to haunt her. 'Go to Amersham...go to the Hall,' her mother had whispered. Then, tortured breaths later, 'Rich, powerful – will look after you.' Amersham she had discovered easily enough, but who was rich and powerful? Who would look after her and why? For days she had pondered that question. Whoever it was, Grainne had trusted him to save her daughter from the poor house, else she would not have willed Elinor to make this journey. But why, then, had there been such long years of silence between them? Perhaps he was elderly, she'd speculated, unable to travel or reclusive, wanting no communication. Or perhaps – and the thought caught at her – he had some connection to the dead father of whom her mother refused to speak. Whatever she'd imagined had proved a mirage. There was no elderly gentleman in need of company, no recluse to be won over. The owner of this rambling pile was a duke, a man not yet thirty, who entertained the premier prince of the land.

⌒

At last the day came to its close. Exhausted by the unfamiliar hard labour, Elinor trudged back along the path which led to the servants' quarters. The light was already fading and she had to pick her way carefully along the narrow track. She was just rounding the last bend, her mind empty with fatigue, when she found herself walking straight into the duke. It seemed he had been riding for he was dressed still in breeches and top boots and carried a whip. But what was he doing here? The stables lay at the other side of the house and this path led only to the dairy.

She stepped hastily to one side to allow him to pass. 'I beg pardon, Your Grace, I did not see you.' Already she was beginning to adopt a servant's cringe, she thought.

'Nor I you, Mistress Milford. Dusk has come early tonight.'

They stood for a moment, caught in each other's gaze, unable or unwilling to move forward. Then he glanced back along the path he had come. 'I must not keep you. You will be wanting your supper.'

That was her cue. She should have scurried away, but something stayed her footsteps. 'Did you wish to see Martha? If you go now, you should catch her. I left her only minutes ago putting away the last of the jugs.'

For a moment he seemed discomfited. 'In that case I should not interrupt her. I think it must be a long day in the dairy.'

'Particularly if you are unused to the work – though I'm sure I shall soon become accustomed.'

'I imagine you will, but what was your former occupation?' He was interesting himself beyond the call of duty, but it was for courtesy's sake only, she told herself.

'I sold goods.' She was deliberately vague. 'A little less tiring than making butter and cream.'

'So why do you no longer sell goods?'

'There is a simple answer, Your Grace. Times are difficult and there are fewer people to buy.'

She hoped that would put a stop to further questions, but she had underestimated him.

'But why choose a dairy?'

'I have had some experience,' she was quick to say, 'and if I satisfy, it will be secure work.'

'I'm sure you will – satisfy, I mean.'

He was standing very close to her, as close as he had been this morning, and there was the same imperious tone to his voice. Imperious but with a hint of devilry. The apologetic duke had vanished – this was one to be wary of again. Had he in fact been going to the dairy to see her, she wondered, rather than Martha? She turned pink at the notion. The sooner this uncomfortable interview ended, the better.

'I must not keep you, sir,' she prompted.

'I think you mean that *I* must not keep *you*,' he returned. 'Go then, Nell Milford.'

She gave a swift curtsy and hurried along the path, aware of his gaze following her. This morning he had looked at her in the same intent fashion and her skin had prickled beneath his gaze. No doubt that was a duke's privilege, to look his fill at female servants. She dreaded to think what other privileges he might claim if he liked what he saw. But his interest in her was simple curiosity, she was sure, for she was not the duke's taste. Most definitely she was not to his taste. She had earlier caught a glimpse of several of his women guests. One in particular – Lady Letitia Vine, Martha had told her with a snort of contempt – wore a painted face and the most outrageously revealing dress. She could never rival such a woman and she thanked heaven it was so.

Chapter Three

'I dunno where they found yer, but it weren't from no dairy.'

Elinor had hoped to make a better impression on her second day but Martha was standing watching her, arms akimbo and brow creased with suspicion, while the younger woman clumsily squeezed excess buttermilk from the mixture.

She picked up the heavy wooden pats and with difficulty began wielding them to shape the butter. Martha's frown deepened.

'I'm not used to these particular pats,' Elinor excused herself.

She had been at work several hours and already her limbs were screaming with pain. She was discovering that making the occasional block of butter for two was a very different prospect to supplying a vast household.

'And my arms are still tired from carrying a heavy valise from Steyning. The stage put me down at the White Horse and it's a good five mile walk from there.'

Her mentor merely snorted and bid her work more quickly.

It was not until they were scouring pails, pats and moulds some hours later that Elinor ventured to speak again. The head dairymaid had been at Amersham her entire working life and it was possible that she rather than the duke might hold the answers Elinor sought.

'The duke is very young to have succeeded to his title,' she began.

'Put more salt in the water,' was all Martha would offer. 'Else we'll 'ave the butter stickin'.'

'I've always thought of dukes as old men,' she pursued, hoping her obvious stupidity would unleash her companion's tongue. It did.

'Dukes is young, old, ugly, 'ansome. This 'un is young and 'ansome. And reckliss.' A rough noise escaped Martha which Elinor took to be a laugh.

'Aren't all young men reckless?' she asked guilelessly.

'Mebbe, but this 'un has the devil riding 'im and that's a fact.'

'In what way?' Martha's willingness to talk was unusual and Elinor seized the moment.

'Drinkin' and gamblin' and carousin' with that no good crowd.' The older woman shook her head irritably. 'It ain't right, not for a duke it ain't.'

'How long has he been duke?'

'Two year – that were when 'is uncle took a toss. Tried to jump too 'igh and broke 'is neck,' she finished in answer to Elinor's unspoken question.

'That must have been felt a great tragedy on the estate.'

'Nah. A bit of a tartar 'e were, though my mum allus said 'e were different as a boy.'

'Your mother worked here?'

'Nigh on thirty year,' Martha said proudly, 'right 'ere in this dairy. Taught me everythin' I know'd. She 'ad the sharpest pair of 'ands, fair box yer ears if yer didn't mind 'er, but she were the neatest butter maker in all Sussex.'

'The old duke sounds very different from his nephew.'

'Mebbe, mebbe not. 'E weren't none too pure as a young 'un either.'

Elinor looked questioningly at her mentor. 'Stories,' Martha said in a harsh whisper.

'There's always gossip.'

'Not gossip,' she said firmly. 'Scandal. Big scandal – a woman, o' course. Some furriner or other. But it were 'ushed up. So don't you go talking.'

'I won't,' Elinor made haste to reassure her.

'Yer better not. It'd be more than me job's worth. Claremonts own most of the county and nobody tangles with 'em.'

It was the longest conversation Elinor had had with her fellow servant and the effort seemed temporarily to exhaust them both. Silence reigned except for the clattering of pans and pails. Martha's testimony raised more questions than it answered, but the wall of silence she'd painted was intriguing. Amersham appeared to be a place of secrets. The reference to a foreign woman hung tantalisingly in the air for though she knew little of her mother's past, Grainne had once confided that as a young girl she had fled her family in Ireland. Would not an Irish woman seem foreign to one who had never ventured further than her birth place?

She was clinging to straws. She knew nothing of her

family's history and Grainne, who had kept silent for so long, could not now fill the gaps. She must try to fill them for herself. She must withstand whatever mockery these so-called noblemen flung at her until she had searched for some trace of herself, of her mother, in this place. She had no idea where to start and thought it unlikely she would succeed. But she must try. Tonight, though, she was bone weary. Two long days in the dairy had succeeded the hardships of a difficult journey. Tonight she would seek her bed the minute she had eaten.

~

Supper was over and she made for the small bedroom she shared with Tilly, one of the kitchen maids. Once out of the servants' hall, she took a right turn, imagining she was walking towards the back staircase which led directly to the top floor of the house. But she was mistaken and instead found herself in the Great Hall. It was huge. Dark oak panelling might have given it a sombre look but for a cupola of coloured glass at the very top of the building three floors up, which allowed the evening light to flood the space, glinting off the suits of armour stationed around its walls and creating pools of golden light here and there on the flagstones. She was entranced and instead of turning back she walked slowly around the enormous space. Portraits lined the walls, dead Claremonts, she assumed. She came to rest at the two largest paintings. They were of a Charles and Louisa Claremont and the severity of their faces startled her. From out of a dark backdrop two pairs of black eyes stared coldly beneath two pairs of black brows. The white curls of their wigs, oddly old-fashioned now, seemed

21

the sole relief from the portraits' unremitting gloom. Even their rich clothes were muted in hue. She looked at the line of writing beneath their names: *Painted on the occasion of their marriage, November 1794.* If that was how they looked on their wedding day, how did their marriage ever prosper?

She should have left then and scuttled back to the safety of the servants' area. Charles and Louisa had just one message for her and it was that she didn't belong where she stood. But an enormous spiral staircase at the end of the hall was too tempting. It wound its sinuous pathway in a double helix through the whole height of the building. Would it not be helpful to know something of the layout of the house? She tiptoed up the staircase to the first floor and was met by a battalion of doors. The first three or four proved to be cupboards or led to unused spaces, but further along the corridor a door stood open. From a brief glance she could see it was a drawing room. The next door displayed a helpful label which told her it was the Music Room. The final door was shut and unlabelled.

Very slowly she opened it a few inches and realised immediately that the room was a library – a very large library – full of books but empty of inhabitants. She was about to slip into the room when a noise from the hall below made her jump back and flatten herself against the corridor's wood panelling, but it was only Mr Jarvis chivvying an idle footman. She let out her breath; she had been so gripped by her exploration she hadn't known she was holding it. The scare had been a reminder, though, that she needed to proceed much more cautiously. Swiftly she retraced her path, intent on regaining the servants' hall as quickly as possible.

'Are you lost, Nell?' It was the butler who materialised at her side as she regained the bottom stair.

She tried to keep her voice calm. 'I must have taken a wrong turning, Mr Jarvis.'

'This part of the house is out of bounds to any but house servants and then only between certain hours.' His voice was coldly severe, punishment if not dismissal lurking in every syllable. She waited to hear her fate, but rescue was to come from an unexpected quarter.

'Jarvis, where are those damn deeds? They need to be with the lawyers – now!'

Gabriel Claremont erupted into the hall from a room at its furthest end, his hand combing an agitated path through already rumpled hair. Close fitting fawn breeches and glossy top boots were his sole concession to formality. A waistcoat of blue embroidered silk was left unbuttoned to reveal the frilled white shirt loosely cloaking his tall frame. In his half-dressed state, he looked little more than a boy, she thought. A small jolt disturbed the measured rhythm of her heart.

The butler's severity vanished and harassment took its place. 'Hannah took them to the study, Your Grace, and placed them on your desk. She found them in the library while dusting.'

'Dusting!' Gabriel's voice bounced off the flagstones. 'Important legal papers – and they are to be at the mercy of a housemaid's cloth!'

'The documents were found beneath the family Bible, Your Grace. There is a deal of paper stored in the room and the book had been used as a weight.'

Gabriel strode furiously towards him. 'A deal of paper which that rascally bailiff was supposed to organise months ago. Where is the villain?'

'I believe Mr Joffey is visiting Hurstwood to oversee the renovations.' If the butler was trying to soothe the situation, it did not appear to be working. Gabriel's expression was unrelenting. 'The property your late uncle left to Mr Roland?' Jarvis added hopefully.

'I know what Hurstwood is, dammit, and I've no interest. Meanwhile I'm left poking around this mausoleum trying to find deeds which will allow Pargiter to buy the fields his family has been renting for centuries. It's not good enough.'

'No, Your Grace. I quite see that. Allow me to search your study.'

'You'll be wasting your time.'

'A minute only, Your Grace.'

Gabriel shrugged his shoulders in irritation and began to retrace his steps when he became aware of Elinor standing silently beneath the portraits of Charles and Louisa.

'Nell? Nell Milford? Are you not a little far from home? Or were you intending to set up a dairy in my hall?' He moved closer and she felt the warmth of his body filling the space between them.

He looked up at the portraits hanging above her head and grimaced. 'Or is it perhaps that you are transfixed by my family history?' He made an expansive gesture with his right arm. 'Allow me to introduce you, Nell. I give you Uncle Charles and Aunt Louisa.'

She followed his glance and a shudder traced its way down her spine.

'Terrifying, aren't they?' he asked genially. 'But not half as terrifying as they were alive.'

She was unsure how to reply since her menial position made it impossible to express her true feelings. 'They are... uncompromising,' she managed at last.

'And *you* are a diplomat, Nell. But be honest. How would you like that pair hanging in your house? You should be thankful you have no hall in which to hang your ancestors.'

'I have no ancestors either,' she replied composedly, 'at least none I know of.'

'No ancestors? You have no family?'

Once more he seemed genuinely interested. His blue eyes, almost sapphire in colour, were fixed on her face and she felt another uncomfortable jolt. What was he doing talking to her like this? It was unfair. She was the dairymaid and should not be mixing with a duke – or with his attractions.

'I have no family living that I know of,' she amended.

'Then we are in the same case.'

Should she remind him he had a cousin and an aunt, housed just yards away? She thought not. It was as though Roland and his mother did not exist for him.

With barely a pause, he spoke again. 'Do you consider it a blessing or a sadness? Having no family, I mean.'

'A sadness, Your Grace, an infinite sadness.'

His expression softened at her words and she was emboldened to ask, 'And you?'

He looked back at the portraits once more and then

gazed past them as though he would bore through the oak panelling to a world beyond. When he spoke, his tone was dull with weariness.

'One cannot choose one's family. On balance I would say it's a blessing.'

'Your Grace, I have the papers here.' Jarvis bustled importantly towards them. 'Hannah placed them underneath the blotter, foolish girl. I will arrange for them to be despatched to the lawyers in Brighton without delay.'

Then noticing that Elinor was still where she should not be, the butler made haste to excuse the lapse. 'Please forgive this intrusion, Your Grace. The girl is new and does not know her way around. Leaving the servants' hall, she inadvertently took the wrong turning.'

Gabriel smiled faintly. 'Don't we all at some time or another?'

He turned back towards his study and Jarvis shooed Elinor through the door into the servants' passageway.

⌒

As the week wore on, she began to find the work less onerous. Martha might have a sharp tongue, but she was good hearted and with her help Elinor was becoming skilled enough to earn her mentor's qualified praise.

'I'll give it yer. Yer may not be as fast as Letty but yer neater. And yer don't waste time flirtin' with them that's above yer touch.'

It was fortunate, Elinor reflected, that she was used to domestic work. Fortunate, too, that the girl whose job she had taken had never arrived. From a young age Nell had been given charge of the Bath household, spending her days cooking and cleaning, helping Grainne to mix paints, buy supplies and spread the word to bring in new customers for her mother's delicately painted miniatures. She had given little thought to the future – not, that is, until that desperate January day when Grainne had returned from delivering her latest commission, soaked and shivering. There had been no money for a doctor, no money for nourishing food or even for warmth during what had been the bitterest winter for years, and a severe chill had quickly turned to pneumonia. But she must not allow sadness to overcome her; she was here for a purpose, to carry out Grainne's last wish.

Her final task of the day was to load two churns of milk onto a small cart and trundle them to the kitchens. The cart was too cumbersome to use the footpath and she was forced to drag it part of the way along the main drive. As she walked, yesterday's conversation with Martha replayed in her mind. The evidence that her mother had ever been at Amersham was the flimsiest. A foreign woman, Martha had said, but how significant was that? Her mother's Irish origin was no more than a story after all.

And while she had leapt at the idea that the previous duke might be the man of Grainne's dying words, the evidence for that was even flimsier. He wasn't the only rich and powerful man to inhabit Amersham Hall, she was sure. There was the present duke's father for a start. And there might be cousins or children of cousins. It was an enormous house and any number of people could have lived here eighteen years ago. She would get nothing more from Martha, she knew, and questioning the august Mr

Jarvis, the only other servant likely to have been here at the time, was laughable. He was less approachable even than the master he served. His affronted expression when he had recovered Gabriel's lost papers still made her smile.

Her heartbeat quickened slightly. Jarvis had mentioned a family Bible. Might that hold a clue? It was the custom to inscribe in the book the names of every member of a family. The Claremont dynasty must be vast, but the Bible might just contain a clue as to whom she should seek. Was it worth the risk of searching for it? She recalled those last few hours of her mother's life: the hot, paper-thin skin of her hands, the hoarse whispers as Grainne used every mite of her remaining breath to help her daughter. It had to be worth it.

She had reached the point where the drive divided, the main carriageway continuing towards the gravelled crescent fronting the house and a narrower one bending towards the servants' quarters. As she took this left fork, she heard the crunch of footsteps and in a moment was overtaken by Roland Frant.

'How are you settling in, Nell?' he asked genially.

'Very well, sir.' She remembered to bob the expected curtsy.

'A little better when the house is quiet, I wager.'

Amersham had been at peace that day since Gabriel's entire party had descended on Worthing, a quiet and dowdy seaside town nearby. She flushed at his mention of the teasing she'd suffered but said stoutly, 'I am sure I will grow accustomed. It is only that Amersham Hall is very different from my last place of work.' That was certainly true.

'I'm sure it is.' His tone was unexpectedly heated. 'It couldn't fail to be with a hedonist at the helm encouraging every kind of corrupt and lewd behaviour.'

She came to a halt, astonished to hear him speak so of his cousin.

'You refer to the duke, I collect.' She wasn't at all sure she had heard him aright.

'You may think it strange I should speak thus of such a near relative, but Gabriel Claremont has succeeded to an office to which he is ill suited. He would have done far better to remain a soldier. I'm sure I don't have to warn you to be on your guard. Any comely girl is a target for him, servant or no servant.'

She flushed hotly and made haste to turn the conversation. 'I had no idea His Grace once served in the army.'

'Indeed, yes. Enlisted as did many peep-o'day boys. But his brother made sure he received a commission soon after he joined the ranks.'

'He has a brother?' This was turning out to be a most surprising exchange.

'No longer, I fear. Jonathan Claremont was killed two years ago. Hence Gabriel's unholy succession.'

He seemed at last to become aware that tittle-tattle with a servant was hardly dignified and hurried to bid her farewell. 'I must allow you to finish your work. Tomorrow is race day and likely to be very busy for you all.' A brief nod and he was gone.

He is angry, Elinor thought, for some reason too angry to consider the impropriety of speaking so to a servant. His tongue had run on in a way that she found unbecoming, but he was a pleasant enough man and evidently wished her well. She must not be too quick to judge him.

And he had given her something to think of. Tomorrow was race day, he'd said, so might that provide her with the opportunity she needed? Every evening loud laughter spilled through the entire house and there was a constant milling of guests from room to room, floor to floor. It would be foolish to attempt to look for the family Bible while the household was awake since it would almost certainly result in instant discovery. And since the guests rarely sought their beds until the early hours, she would have to forgo any idea of sleep if she were to search the library at night. But tomorrow might be different. A long day in the open air might end with the house party sufficiently fatigued to retire before midnight. She could only hope.

Chapter Four

The first of June dawned clear and bright. A race course had been constructed towards the southern boundary of the Amersham land in the months when Gabriel had first returned to a grieving household, a time when he was desperate for distraction. Amersham Hall sat atop an incline and to the south of the house the land fell away, at first gently and then far more precipitously. It allowed the Hall magnificent views over the surrounding landscape – fields, woods, and shimmering in the distance, the South Downs – but it meant, too, that a race course which navigated such a steep incline was a trial for both horses and jockeys. The duke's guests found this hugely entertaining since gambling on winners and losers was even more of a lottery than usual. Today the duke was running his favourite horse, Emperor, while the Prince Regent had pinned his colours on Pegasus, a rare palomino he had bought at great expense from Sir John Lade.

A generous swathe of the local gentry had been invited to the meeting and had entered their own favourite horses in the various races. From noon conveyances of every kind – broughams, landaulets, elegant barouches and even a dashing high-perch phaeton or two – began to roll towards the house and deposit their inhabitants at the Hall's imposing entrance. The duke had ordered a light lunch before ferrying his neighbours and house guests by carriage down to the race course. A few chose to walk and drifted to the meeting on foot along a path mown through the meadow, with bunting strung between the trees on either side. The atmosphere was noisy and excited, one of carnival, setting the lower pastures of the estate ablaze with silks and satins of every colour.

The races were about to start when Elinor received an urgent summons from Mr Jarvis to attend him in the kitchen. The race course was situated on the other side of the house and she had thought herself safe in the dairy from any unwanted attention, but the butler's first words put paid to that hope.

'We will need you here this afternoon, Nell. Martha can attend to the dairy. Since we are accommodating far more guests than expected, I shall require additional pairs of hands.'

His wintry face gave little away, but it was clear he was severely vexed. 'There are insufficient footmen to cover the situation. James and Thomas have been given leave of absence – a regrettable lack of foresight – and Henry has taken to his bed with a fever. Or so he says.' There was a loud sniff. 'We must make do with women.'

'But I have never waited at table.' Elinor could feel the trap closing, but escape was impossible. The butler's response was sharp.

'You will not be required to wait at table, merely to pass

among the guests with the refreshments that His Grace considers necessary for the meeting.'

The housekeeper bustled into the kitchen at that moment and brought the dialogue to a decisive close. She carried a stack of white pinafores and fresh lace caps. 'Jane, Elsa, Becky and you, Nell Milford. Put these on.'

If Elinor could have run, she would have done so, but knowing she must keep her job she had no option but to obey. All four girls donned starched aprons and caps and allowed Mr Jarvis to marshal them into line. One by one they were handed large trays filled to overflowing with an array of small but beautifully fashioned appetisers.

'Go, go now!'

Mrs Lucas's voice was urgent, ushering them out of the kitchen and through the narrow passageway to the side door. From here a long walk over manicured lawns led eventually to the rougher pasture of the race course. 'And come back when the tray is empty,' the housekeeper called after them. 'There will be others waiting for you.'

It was well the recent heavy work had increased Elinor's physical strength since by the time she reached the lower reaches of the meadow, the silver platter she carried had turned to lead. She was intent on lightening her burden as quickly as possible and, caring little for delicate sensibilities, lost no time in thrusting the tray beneath as many noses as she could find. The ladies brushed her aside, but the men were made of sterner stuff and ate with a will.

On her return to the kitchen she saw Roland Frant in the distance strolling towards the course. His resentment of his cousin evidently did not prevent him attending. An older woman was by his side, dour and unsmiling, and bearing the same family resemblance she had noticed in Roland.

Over the next few hours Elinor ferried platter after platter from kitchen to meadow and had barely begun to rid herself of the latest clutch of delicacies when the duke, fresh from Emperor's success in winning the meeting's Gold Cup, hailed her from a distance.

'Did you take another wrong turning, Nell, or is it that you've gone up in the world?'

He strolled towards at a leisurely pace. For once he easily matched his fashionable guests in elegance. She tried not to notice how attractive he looked, but could not prevent her eyes resting on his athletic form. His blue tailcoat was a perfect fit, its gilt buttons catching the sun and flashing fire, while beneath the coat a blue and grey striped silk waistcoat lightened the formality. A starched neckcloth in pure white linen completed the ensemble, tied in a pristine *trône d'amour* and just grazing his chin.

He bent over her tray. 'Let me celebrate your meteoric rise to footman by eating one of your pastries.'

'It is a passing rise only, Your Grace.' Then unable to stop herself she added, 'I would have preferred to remain in the dairy.'

'Surely not! Not when you can witness my horse win by a length, and serve such delightful people as these!' He gestured mockingly towards his guests, scattered in groups across the meadow, but all drinking copiously and talking loudly at each other.

'Many would consider butter making more useful.' She

was unwilling to be cajoled.

'But then this is a meeting of the use*less*. And these pointless pieces of pastry,' he waved at Elinor's tray, 'seem perfectly suited to such a gathering, wouldn't you say?'

'I am a servant, Your Grace. I do not have opinions.'

'That I doubt. Nor that you would voice them if you chose. Your face is too expressive, Mistress Milford. It clearly speaks disgust.'

'Not disgust, Your Grace. Pain. This tray weighs very heavy.'

'Then let me show you how useful *I* can be.' And before she realised what he was about, he had taken the tray from out of her hands. 'Let me show you how capable I am at serving my guests, even though I'm incapable of much else. Who knows, I might even gain your approval.'

She flushed with annoyance at the way he had turned the tables on her, but he was speaking again. 'Tell me, why is it that you *aren't* in the dairy?'

'Mr Jarvis was desperate. It seems he is bereft of footmen and has been forced to make do with women.' She tried to keep her face solemn, but a crease slowly formed at the corner of her wide mouth.

'Poor Jarvis,' he mourned, a grin lighting his face. 'A butler's life is not a happy one.'

'There you are! At last! I've been looking for you everywhere.'

The woman Elinor had glimpsed on her first day at Amersham bounced into view and ignoring the platter Gabriel carried, thrust her arm possessively into his. She was dressed even less modestly than her fellows in a low-cut gown of turquoise satin, her face a little too rouged and her hair a little too bejewelled.

Quite suddenly she became aware of the tray Gabriel held and let go of his arm.

'What are you doing, Duke? You look almost to be one of your servants!'

'There are worst fates, Letitia. Come, we must move among our guests,' and he made to usher her away.

'Nonsense, Gabriel. Here girl, take this.' And Letitia Vine wrenched the tray from his hands and almost threw it at Elinor.

'Can I interest you in a lobster patty, your ladyship?' Elinor asked, her face a mask of innocence.

The older woman shuddered exaggeratedly and waved her away. 'Remove the tray at once. Pastries, whatever next!'

The woman was ridiculous. 'Next?' she responded guilelessly. 'Next I believe is a fruit mousse.'

Letitia Vine glared at her. 'I do not wish to eat at all, you stupid girl.'

'Then I cannot imagine why I have been offering you this tray. I am indeed stupid.'

The woman turned a violent red and Elinor was unable to prevent her mouth quivering with amusement.

'Are you laughing at me, girl?'

'Why ever would I do that, milady?'

'Your servant, Duke, is insubordinate,' Letitia hissed. 'You should rid your household of her. At the very least, Mrs Lucas should have trained her better.'

'Nell works in the dairy under the tutelage of Martha,' he said indifferently, and took the woman's arm in another attempt to usher her away. But Lady Vine was having none of it.

'A dairymaid! Good God! What are you doing allowing such a rough creature to serve your guests?'

'There has been a little domestic difficulty. Nell will soon be returning to her dairy.'

He was reminding her where she belonged, she thought, and felt anger begin to burn a fierce path. But she dared not let her feelings show and forced herself to drop a small curtsy.

'Beg pardon, milady,' she managed, with downcast eyes, before turning away and heading in the direction of the kitchen. As she turned she became aware of the puzzlement on Gabriel's face, but she was too upset to dwell on it.

⁓

The duke listened with less than half an ear to his companion's string of complaints – they were likely to prove no more engaging than the lady's compliments. Letitia Vine seldom said anything interesting and even more rarely said anything true, but in this instance she was hitting the nail squarely on the head. Nell Milford *was* insubordinate, but why he could not begin to fathom. There was a mystery attached to the dairymaid he had acquired from nowhere, and he wanted to solve it. She bothered him. Not just her lovely face and figure, though they were distraction enough, but her whole demeanour. She did as she was commanded, but with a marked reluctance. She answered back. She looked directly at her superiors. She was certainly unusual. She might wear a little grey mouse dress, but he was sure she was anything but. When she felt herself unobserved, those wonderful misty green eyes could be sharply appraising and the wide generous mouth tremble with humour. She was something other than she professed, he would put his life on it.

~

In her agitation Elinor elbowed her way through the crowd of racegoers unconcerned whether or not they wished to eat the delicacies she carried. She was sick of being spoken to as though she hardly existed, sick of her dignity reduced to tatters. The meeting was almost at an end and she had the kitchen in her sights. She would return straight to the house and divest herself of tray and uniform. In her rush to get there she stumbled over a tuft of rough grass and landed, complete with platter, in the arms of a gentleman she had never before seen. Calling him rotund would be kind, she thought, for he had almost burst through the maroon tailcoat he wore, its large mother of pearl buttons straining alarmingly. His breeches, if anything, were even tighter and he breathed heavily as he took her full weight.

Immediately, one of his companions came forward and set her roughly on her feet. 'Watch where you're walking, you clumsy girl.' Elinor was pushed forcefully to one side.

'Leave her be, Lansley. It was an accident.' The voice was peculiarly sweet for such a very large man.

'But Your Highness –'

'No, no, it was an accident, wasn't it, my dear?'

She nodded, slightly out of breath from her rampage up the field, but also a little overawed. This had to be the Prince Regent and she had almost sat on him.

'And what have you there?'

The Prince came closer and breathed heavily on her. He smelt of spirits and a very strong perfume. She recoiled, but tried to keep the tray outstretched between them. The Regent's plump, be-ringed hand hovered for a moment and then swooped down to scoop a lobster patty from the plate. 'Ah, a neat little delicacy, like the person who carries them.'

She turned bright red and bowed her head. Was there to be no end to the humiliations of the afternoon?

'No need to colour up, my dear. You are a beauty. She's a beauty, ain't she Lansley?'

Lansley did not reply, but with an impatient signal waved her away. She needed no prompting, hurriedly backing from the royal presence and making for the house. The kitchen maids were still elbow deep in washing china, but not a morsel of food remained and Elinor was dismissed at last. Ignoring the tantalising smell coming from the great range, she abandoned the idea of taking supper and went directly to her room. Eating was the last thing on her mind. It had been a hateful afternoon. She had hated the uniform, hated the heavy trays she had been forced to carry, but most of all she had hated the duke's guests. And the Prince Regent! She had heard tales of his womanising, but had thought him too old and indeed too fat for them to be true. But apparently not. Even a humble maidservant was not safe from his attentions.

She lay on her bed and tried to block from her mind the events of the day. In particular she had no wish to think of Lady Letitia Vine and her plunging *décolleté*. The incident with that overblown lady had been by far the most humiliating. She could discount her aching limbs since she had grown accustomed to physical fatigue. She was even growing accustomed to the casual discourtesies of those she served, but it was the duke's sharp reminder of her station that continued to rankle. The woman was no doubt his *chère-amie* and he had been trying to appease her. Elinor did not admire his choice and was at a loss to understand why he would wish to make such a woman his mistress. For all his arrogance, he was infinitely the superior. It wasn't only that he was a handsome man. There were several in his party more handsome. It wasn't that he possessed a great position and the wealth that accompanied it. It was something indefinable that set him apart from the flotsam with whom he floated. She saw it in his eyes, the quick intelligence, the wry humour, but also a deep, ineffable sadness. Those intense blue eyes said so much and she wondered if she were alone in reading their message.

An overwhelming weariness took hold and in minutes she slept. It was much later that she was shaken awake by Tilly, asking her if she wished to join her fellows at The King's Head. Fresh from their triumphs on the race course, the duke and his guests had decided to stage impromptu charades and after dinner had ordered several boxes of old clothes to be brought down from the attics to the drawing room. Most of the servants had been dismissed and told they were not wanted that evening. The majority had decided on a convivial gathering at the village inn, the remainder to snatch some additional rest. Elinor turned down the invitation with a sleepy smile, but behind closed eyes her mind was already ticking. The great house was likely to be very quiet. This would be her chance, she decided.

Chapter Five

Every one of the duke's guests, it seemed, was in the drawing room intent on diversion and she was unlikely to encounter any stray wanderer. Already the noise was raucous and judging by the amount of wine she had seen a footman take up earlier, it could only get more so. She would easily hear the merrymaking from the library, and once it grew quieter it would be time to leave since it would mean the party was breaking up.

Once she was sure the coast was clear she slipped out of her attic bedroom and down to the first floor, using the servants' staircase. She encountered nobody. The drawing room door was shut but the revellers' shrieks and shouts were clearly audible. That was all to the good. She opened the library door a few inches and was met by a solid, impenetrable darkness. For a moment she was blind, but once inside the room she was able to light the candle she had taken from those which stood ready for the nightly use of guests and position it carefully on the highest of several occasional tables.

By its light she could see the task that awaited her. Stacks of paper tottered untidily in all four corners of the room.

They were an unlikely resting place for what she sought, and after a brief glance she discounted them. If the family Bible had been used as a paperweight, it must now have been reshelved by Hannah. Where to find it amidst this welter of books? Long windows filled one wall of the room, but the remaining three were crammed with volumes from ceiling to floor. Without exception the books looked very old and very untouched. A family Bible should surely have pride of place, but from her slow survey of the room it seemed not. There had been an attempt at organisation: the books were shelved first according to their content and then alphabetically. She perused the different categories. Would History be the most obvious place to start? Yes, she would start with History and make her way through the whole section from A to Z.

It was a tiresome business since the gilt lettering on each spine had been rubbed away and she was forced to open every book to see its contents. After an hour of lifting down volumes and re-shelving them, her shoulders ached and her dress was filthy. The books had not been handled for years and she was in constant danger of choking from a pall of dust. When one very large cloud engulfed her she tried desperately to stifle her sneeze but failed, the sound seeming to reverberate through the entire house. She crept to the library door and listened, her heart beating a tattoo. But the laughter across the corridor continued unabated.

Back to the shelves. This time she began work on the Reference section, reasoning that after History this was the most likely place. The books here proved even heavier and no more forthcoming. With a sigh she moved on and found herself facing a label marked Travel. An unlikely home for a Bible, but at least the section was modest in size. One book caught her eye -*Tales of Rajasthan* – and she began to read, more for the interlude it offered her aching arms than from any real interest. But it proved a fascinating journal and she found herself caught up in the traveller's strange experiences in a country of which she knew little. She had just torn herself away from this intriguing account and begun to search haphazardly through the remaining shelves when she became aware that the noise from the drawing room had stopped. In fact she feared it might have stopped some time ago.

Hastily she made for the door and inadvertently sent the nearest stack of paper toppling to the floor. She bent to scrabble the scattered sheets together and there right before her – the very book she sought. The Bible appeared to have been thrown untidily on the heap of papers and then covered with more. Her body brisked with excitement and her hands shook, as with the greatest of care she turned the pages, yellow-edged and spotted with age. One page, two pages, the family tree! The first name shining out at her was Gabriel's. He was twenty-six years old, she calculated, young for a man who had seen so much war and death at first hand. And there was his brother beside him, his birth followed by the sombre record of his death. The quill seemed to have stuttered at this point, for the ink grew thick and uneven. A new hand had written the next entry: Charles Claremont's passing, as Martha had said, a mere two years previously. His age made him a contemporary of her mother, she noted neutrally. But then looking more closely, she saw that the name of his wife, Louisa, had been scratched out with an almost fierce pleasure. Was Louisa dead? It seemed unlikely though Elinor had heard no mention of her since she had come to Amersham. But divorce was even less likely. So why had Charles' wife been obliterated so brutally? And was it significant that Louisa had not borne a single child?

The family was a great deal smaller than she had imagined. What of Hugo Claremont, Gabriel's father, and those missing cousins she had supposed to exist? There was just one – Roland. His father and Gabriel's had died when their sons were very small, years before she herself was born. Neither could be the man her mother intended. No, there was only one person of the right age who had lived at Amersham eighteen years ago, a person bereft of heirs and eventually it seemed bereft of a wife. And that was Charles Claremont, fourth Duke. What connection could her mother have to him? A scandal, the air whispered. Is that why her mother had fled to Bath? A scandal involving Elinor's father and this man, Charles. Is that why, as she'd always presumed, her father had died or disappeared before he could reach Bath? *The Claremonts own most of this county, you don't mess with them*, had been Martha's warning. She felt herself grow cold. But if Charles Claremont had somehow been implicated in her father's disappearance, he would surely be the last person Grainne would want her child to find. Yet the ghostly echo of her mother's words was with her even now – *powerful, rich* – and the duke had certainly been that.

She was indulging in a flight of fancy, nothing more.

Her quest had come to a full stop and the fact hit her hard. She had been so sure the family Bible would tell her what she wanted to know. It hadn't and she must live with the consequences. Her only security was her work as a dairymaid and she was likely to lose even that if she were found here. She wetted her fingers and snuffed out the candle. Thank goodness none of the guests had seen its faint beam of light when they'd left for an unusually early bedtime.

Still clutching her candlestick, she slipped around the library door and closed it very quietly behind her. She must regain the back staircase as soon as possible.

'And what pray are you doing in this part of the house?' The voice was at her elbow and she spun around.

Gabriel Claremont leant carelessly against the panelled walls, but his expression was far from careless. He moved the candle he held closer to her face and she blinked in its sudden illumination.

'Have you lost your tongue, Nell, as well as your way?'

'No, Your Grace.' She kept her voice meek. She had once more been found trespassing and now was the time to think on her feet. 'I am sorry, Your Grace, but I could not sleep and wished for something to read. I thought it would not matter if I took no books.'

His annoyance turned to amusement. 'Something to read – from the Amersham library?' She nodded.

'Did you not know this library is one of the most prestigious in the country? You will have to look elsewhere for your Gothic romance.'

'I do not read Gothic romance,' she exclaimed with indignation, and then more honestly, 'at least only very occasionally.'

'Then what do you read? What possible interest could the Amersham library hold for you?' He moved closer and she was aware of a tingling down her back. She smelt his subtle scent and the warmth of a hard, muscular body.

'History,' she improvised. At least that had been one of the sections she had searched.

'History is a wide brief.' She saw his face in the candlelight, at once laconic and suspicious.

'Classical history,' she said, desperately trying to remember the lessons Grainne had taught her.

'Ah yes, Livy, I imagine.' His tone was sardonic.

'No, not Livy. Cicero,' she countered.

'Wasn't Cicero a philosopher?'

'An historian too, I believe.'

She should not have been goaded into retort, but he was behaving insufferably. She had been foolish to think he would do otherwise. Gabriel Claremont was as arrogant as she had first thought. In the shifting flame of the candle his deep blue eyes appeared almost black. He moved closer and she could feel his breath on her cheek. A strand of hair had fallen forward over his brow and she had to restrain herself from pushing it back. What was she thinking? Here she was in the middle of the night with an angry man standing inches away and all she could think of was what it would feel like to touch him.

He took her chin between his fingers and tipped her face towards his. 'I don't know what you are doing here, Nell, but the main house is out of bounds to you, strictly out of bounds.'

He let go of her and the smile was back on his face. 'Remember that well or when *I* can't sleep I might just visit you in *your* quarters. I'm sure I'd find the experience a great deal more interesting than Cicero.'

She blushed scarlet and was thankful that in the dim light he was unlikely to see the effect he was having. 'May I go now, Your Grace?' She tried to keep her voice steady.

'You may, but next time, Mistress Nell, you won't escape as lightly.'

She fled towards the safety of her attic. The duke was an attractive man, very attractive, seductive even, but he was also a hardened rogue, she was sure. The way he had moved his body so close to hers she could feel his breath, the way he had tipped her face to his so that she had thought at any moment he would bring those warm lips down on hers. She gave herself a mental shake. She must drive such thoughts from her mind; she had had a lucky escape.

She struggled awake as the first rays of light streamed through the attic's uncurtained window. The memory of her abortive mission the previous evening gradually filled her mind and left her feeling dull and deflated. It had all been for nothing. The hard labour, the terror of discovery, and the troubling encounter with the duke. And now she must face yet another day.

By the time she reached the dairy the sun had already begun to climb the sky and touch her skin with its warmth. But she hardly noticed for her mind was once more busy. Last night, even very early this morning, she had been ready to relinquish her quest and settle for the small security she possessed. Further trespass could only put it at risk. But there was a mystery here, she was certain, and something pushed her to uncover it. If Charles had been the man in her mother's thoughts, was it possible she might one day find a connection between him and her parents? The practical evidence for her mother's involvement in Amersham was tenuous, but instinct told her otherwise. She fingered the broken locket she carried, feeling through her skin its almost hypnotic force. What would Grainne want? She had kept her daughter in ignorance, yet in her last painful moments on earth she had tried to make good the years of silence. In the deepest reaches of her heart Elinor knew she would continue the search, no matter what the cost.

Those papers last night – she had barely glanced at them, but she could see they were business communications relating to the estate and its tenants. So were there personal papers elsewhere? Where would Charles have kept his most sensitive documents? A rough plan of the house flickered past her inner eye. A study was the most likely depository and Gabriel's study had doubtless been his uncle's before him. If Charles Claremont had had dealings with her parents, what better place than his own private room to keep those confidences? Judging by the chaos that reigned in the house, any papers were likely to be there to this day. She wondered if Gabriel had any idea of what his study contained and for a few seconds considered telling him why she had come to Amersham. But only for a few seconds. He would almost certainly laugh her out of the gates if she were foolish enough to confess the truth.

There was no help for it. She would have to search

the study secretly, but if she were again caught prying...
she flamed at the thought of the duke's last words and her
usually buoyant spirits failed. She would have to be extra
vigilant and wait for an opportunity when the whole company had vacated the house and was certain to be gone for
many hours.

Chapter Six

Martha left for the kitchen at noon that day, carrying the batch of butter pats they had made that morning, and Elinor began straightway on the now familiar cleaning routine. As she scrubbed the marble shelf that ran beneath one of the double windows, she spied a group of figures coming towards the creamery. They seemed vaguely familiar, particularly the corpulent man who appeared to have been poured into tight cream pantaloons and a tight tail coat of shining blue velvet. A brightly coloured floral waistcoat in startling hues of red completed his ensemble and made Elinor blink even from this distance. It was the Regent. He seemed to have difficulty navigating the flagged path and leant for support on the two men who had accompanied him at the race meeting.

As they drew nearer, the taller of the two called out, 'Hey there, dairy. His Highness needs service.'

Why had Martha chosen this very moment to leave and why, oh why, had she not gone with her?

'Your Royal Highness,' she said, and bobbed a curtsy as she tripped up the steps.

'At last,' the prince wheezed. 'I seem to have walked an age to find you. But I am sure it will be worthwhile. What do you think, Lansley? I wasn't mistaken yesterday. A pretty little darling, eh?'

The man addressed as Lansley bared his teeth in what Elinor imagined was a smile. His gallantry was as unwelcome as his master's.

The prince was muttering almost to himself. 'Mind you, not as buxom as – what was her name – the girl who was here before?'

'Letty, I believe, sir.'

'Yes, Letty. Not as buxom but most comely, wouldn't you say?'

Lansley again bared the awful teeth and the other man gave a high whinnying laugh. Really, if they did not make her feel so uneasy, it would be better than a pantomime. But she was uneasy.

'Let me welcome you to Amersham, my dear,' the prince said grandly, as though he owned the property. Which he probably did, Elinor surmised, having only the haziest notion of Crown privilege. 'And tell me where you have sprung from.' He smiled in a worryingly doting fashion.

'I have come from Bath, Your Highness.'

'Frightful place,' the Regent opined 'The waters taste like a sewer. But you know, I would have said you came from Ireland. That colouring, eh, Franks,' he said to the other man, 'pure Irish.'

The topic seemed exhausted and Elinor was anxious to remind her visitors of their purpose. 'May I bring you a glass of milk, Your Highness?'

The prince let out a roar of laughter which choked itself to a splutter. 'What do you take me for, girl? Milk!'

If he had not come to the dairy to drink milk, what had he come for? It soon became abundantly clear.

'Yes, Claremont has a good eye, I'll give him that. A lovely face and a delightful figure. Heartening to find beauty in such an out of the way place.'

She was now very uncomfortable. The prince seemed to have only one object of interest and the thought made her shudder.

'How would you like to visit the Pavilion, my dear?' George airily tossed the question at her. 'Come as my special guest, eh, Lansley?' And he roared with laughter again.

'I thank you, Your Highness, but I am engaged to work at Amersham Hall.'

'Don't you worry your little head. The duke is a great friend of mine. He'll be more than happy to let you go – may even give you your job back, you know, when the – em – visit is over.'

Now seriously alarmed, Elinor made to step back towards the dairy but the prince instantly shot out his arm and grabbed her round the waist. 'Well, if you won't come to an old man, let an old man come to you.' And he pulled her close to him. She felt his corsets sticking into her flesh and the cloying mix of drink and perfume wash over her. She thought she might be sick.

'Go back to the house, Lansley. You too, Franks. Leave us. We will do very well together, eh, my dear.'

His two companions turned and made their way back along the flagged path, leaving Elinor feeling as panicked as a condemned felon facing the final drum roll. If only Martha would come. But the older woman must have stayed to eat her midday meal and engage in a little gossip. She would not return for at least half an hour. Elinor felt her breath coming short and needed all her strength of mind to refrain from screaming. But then he was pushing her down the steps to the dairy, his bulk filling the doorway. The thunder of her heart had taken over her whole body and she was losing control.

Frantically she caught hold of herself; this was not the time for die-away airs. The thunder was getting louder – not her heart after all but a horse galloping ever closer. The Regent stopped in his tracks, listening. Then a cracking and rustling as grass and branches were pushed aside and a large, glossy chestnut broke through the cover of the trees.

'Your Highness, good day,' a voice hailed.

The Regent turned awkwardly and nearly overbalanced. His face shaded a fiery red. 'Ah, Claremont. There you are. I've been looking for you everywhere.'

'Well, here I am. Are you taking a glass of milk, sir? Not your usual tipple, surely.' Gabriel slid from the horse and advanced. He held out his arm to assist the prince up the dairy steps.

'What a ridiculous suggestion!' The Regent shook himself free of the proffered arm and began climbing towards the path. 'Now I've found you, I shall return to the house.' His tone was petulant. 'When you can spare the time, I need to make arrangements for my departure.'

Gabriel watched the Regent out of sight and then turned back to Elinor, standing motionless in the doorway.

'You seem to have a habit of getting yourself into trouble.'

'That is hardly fair,' she protested. 'I'm guilty of nothing more than trying to do my job – despite others' best efforts.'

'You've a mighty sharp tongue for a dairymaid. Let us hope your prowess at butter making is as keen.'

'If I appear rude, I am sorry. His Highness flustered me.'

Gabriel grinned. 'Prinny tends to have that effect. Cicero doesn't offer too much help in that department, I imagine.'

She flushed at the mention of her last night's escapade. He was looking directly at her, as though trying to read her mind, and she found herself drowning in the intense blue of his eyes. For a moment their glances locked, then he gathered the reins in his hand and swung himself into the saddle. Last night he had appeared almost forbidding, yet today he had risked a powerful prince's displeasure to rescue her. She was still puzzling over this when he vanished in the direction of the stables.

⌒

She must have been scared, Gabriel thought, alone and facing a rampant prince. But she had stayed cool, kept her dignity, even outfaced Prinny. She was decidedly novel. There were plenty of Sirs and Your Graces in her speech, but somehow her whole tone said plainly that she considered herself an equal. Altogether, she was a strange kind of servant. She was also a trespasser. Even if he believed her story last night about seeking a book to read, she should not have been in the library; she must have known that. And did he really believe the faradiddle she'd told? He did not. A dairymaid who read Cicero – it was more than unusual. No, Miss Milford, whoever she was, had arrived at Amersham Park for a purpose and it wasn't to serve milk and make butter. She was playing an underhand game, but he hoped very much it wasn't a nefarious one. He wanted to acquit her of involvement in any real wickedness. He wasn't sure why; his impulse towards gallantry had died on the battlefield. But last night when she'd looked up at him, those hazy green eyes focused by fear, he'd wanted not to reprimand but to comfort.

Riding into the stable courtyard, he threw the reins to one of the under grooms and shouted his instructions. 'Wash her down and look at her left knee, will you. I'll come back later to fix a poultice if it's needed.'

He made a detour through the rose garden to reach his study, avoiding any guests who might be lingering in the Great Hall. Flinging himself headlong on to the scratched leather couch, he lay brooding. Something about her made him itch. It was clear to him he should keep away – she unsettled him too much – but equally clear that today he'd had no choice. He'd had to intervene. He was sure she had the strength of character to beat back a dozen marauding men, but Prinny was something else. When he'd come upon the little tableau he'd felt real anger at this flaccid prince who used his great position to frighten and cajole, and the likely repercussions from embarrassing the Regent had not weighed with him for one moment.

He supposed she had been too great a temptation for George. Forget the dairymaid and she was enticing as a woman. If that black hair were ever released from its severe constraint... And not even the drab, grey gown she wore could entirely hide the curves of a covetable figure. Her eyes, too, were magical, changing with the light and with her mood. She could fire his blood, but he wouldn't let her. Unlike the Prince Regent, he did not look below stairs for his pleasure. There were plenty of women of his own station if he were willing, half a dozen residing at Amersham Hall at this very moment. He wished them all away. And their male counterparts.

What was he doing, he a soldier for four years, consorting with this ragbag of opportunists? The answer, he guessed, was that he no longer cared what happened to him. He would play the Duke of Amersham in Jonathan's place, play at being a figurehead for the family. But it was fustian, a bag of moonshine. None of it meant a jot. Inside he was as dead as the only person he had ever loved.

Chapter Seven

It had been three days since Gabriel Claremont left for Brighton and every morning Elinor wondered if this day would see his return. His intention had been to escort the Regent to his exotic palace by the sea, but the errand seemed to be taking an inordinate time. No doubt he had been tempted by the entertainments on offer though it was wise not to think too much on those. She could only hope that life in Brighton would soon pall since Amersham did not feel right without him. She had become used to seeing his tall figure walking alongside the bailiff, his face a mix of bafflement and boredom, or striding energetically towards the stables, or swinging his team of matched bays around the gravelled crescent to arrive precisely at the front entrance.

It was already Friday and the end of the week would see the village fair in full swing. Every year Martha was asked to prepare a special order of butter and cheese for Amersham Hall's own stand. Since it was intricate work she wanted the dairy to herself and shooed her helper from the door around noon. It gave Elinor a few hours' respite and, though the weather had turned cool, she set off for a brisk tour of the Hall's far reaching grounds.

She must come up with a plan. The duke's absence might have offered an excellent opportunity to raid his study except for his guests who spilled into every room. She wondered what attraction they held for him, a soldier who for years had fought so bravely. Perhaps, for all their ugliness, they helped to fill an emptiness – she could not forget that he'd so recently lost his brother. That was the problem, she scolded herself, she could not get him out of her mind. Gabriel's image danced through her thoughts and the sound of his voice was constantly in her ears. For days she had been unable to shake herself free and she didn't like it.

By the time she was once more in full sight of the house and making her way towards the broad drive, she had given herself entirely to daydreaming and a gentle smile creased the corners of her mouth. Heedless of her surroundings she walked on, only to be almost knocked from her feet by a sudden, powerful rush of air. The wheels of a carriage screeched against the gravel and four steaming bays stumbled to a halt. A lithe figure jumped down from the perch and in a second was at her elbow.

'Do you not think to look where you are walking? I may have ruined my horses' mouths by pulling on them so, and they are expensive beasts.'

The rapid descent from daydream to angry reality shocked her. Gabriel Claremont had once more run her down.

'And do *you* not think you should drive with greater care?' she demanded, as though he occupied no more exalted status than the local carrier.

'I believe you forget yourself.' His tone was even but feathered with ice. He was right – she was in no position to object. She tried to bow her head, but managed it so half-heartedly as to make the gesture almost insulting.

The duke ignored this and nodded at his groom. 'Drive on to the stables, Parsons. I will be with you shortly.' And then to Elinor, 'Enough of this. Are you hurt?' His voice held a kinder note.

'Not in this instance but I would not vouch for your third attempt.' She was unable to keep the angry tremble from her voice.

'My third attempt? What do you speak of?' He was genuinely mystified.

'Only that you appear to make a habit of running me off the road. On the first occasion I was walking a public highway, or so I thought – but perhaps Your Grace owns that, too?'

'Speak plainly, Nell. What exactly did I do to incur your wrath and when?'

'The day I arrived I was forced to leap into the ditch to escape death at your hands.'

'Into the ditch?' His smile was appreciative. 'I wish I'd seen that.'

'Doubtless it would have given you amusement.' The incident still smarted. 'But only if you were likely to notice a person as lowly as myself.'

'Don't be ridiculous. When I'm driving at full speed, I see little to right or left, including dairymaids. If indeed you *are* a dairymaid.'

They were approaching dangerous ground and she thought to walk away, but he caught her arm and pulled her back towards him. 'Not so fast, Mistress Nell. What are you doing here? Should you not be in the dairy at this hour?'

'No, indeed, she said a little too hotly. 'Martha wished to have the place to herself and I was given leave to take exercise in the gardens and beyond.'

'And what is Martha engaged in that is so important?'

'She is preparing for the village fair tomorrow.'

'Ah, yes, I had forgot. The clamour of Brighton tends to push such small pleasures out of mind.'

His grip on her arm had dropped and she hoped she might be allowed to continue on her way. It wasn't so much that she minded his touch, it was the shocking thought that she didn't. But he had not yet finished with her.

'Tell me, how are you faring under Martha's instruction?'

It was an unexpected question, but she tried to answer as honestly as she could. 'I am fortunate in having a good teacher.'

'So you are happy with us?'

It seemed to matter to him. 'I love Amersham.' It was strangely true since she had felt an attachment to the place from the very beginning.

'Do you?' His voice expressed surprise. But surely, she thought, he must care for the estate even more than she. It was his birthplace and his inheritance.

She found herself asking, 'Do *you* not love it?'

'Not greatly. But Amersham is my destiny. I cannot escape it.'

'One can change one's destiny. I believe everyone has that power if they will but try.'

'As you are doing?' Dangerous territory once more and she held her breath. But he didn't pursue the topic. Instead he said in a leaden tone, 'It is my duty, Nell, or so I'm told, to husband the estate and care for its dependants.'

'You are still adjusting to new circumstances,' she ventured. 'You could not have thought such a burden would fall on you.'

'You are right. The burden, as you call it, would have been far better shouldered by my brother. He was born to inherit and trained to be duke. I can only act the role.'

He looked lost, for the moment the devil-may-care man transformed into the boy he must once have been. She wanted to comfort him.

'Amersham must have been a wonderful place to grow up,' she tried.

'Very occasionally.' He still seemed lost in time, looking away to a world she could not envisage, and then quite suddenly he grabbed her arm. 'Come with me, I want to show you something. If you love Amersham as much as you say, it is only right you should know one of its secrets.'

There was no chance to protest before he was dragging her with some force towards the wooded area on the other side of the drive. She had no idea what lay beyond the trees and could only hope the duke was not about to live up to her worst fears. But she need not have worried. He let go of her arm as soon as they stepped onto the shadowy pathway leading through the woods.

'Come,' he beckoned her on.

The path was twisting and uneven, in parts made almost impenetrable by the colonising undergrowth. Elinor was forced to fix her eyes on the forest floor to avoid tripping on tree roots that crooked their way above and beneath the path, or stumbling into the bountiful clusters of nettles and thigh-high weeds. The duke was some way ahead when she heard a slight slithering noise close at hand. She stopped on a sixpence. She was going no further without knowing what exactly was concealed beneath the covering of leaves and stray branches.

Gabriel turned and grinned at her. 'What is it? Can you hear a snake?'

'A snake! And you bring me here!'

'Don't be craven, Nell. They are only grass snakes and won't hurt you one little bit. In fact they're terrified of *you*. On very hot days Jonathan and I would watch them slide through the wood to sunbathe on the rocks. Come, I'll show you.'

He retraced his steps and caught hold of her hand again and she had little option but to go with him. Better certainly than returning alone, whatever the supposed harmlessness of the snakes. They walked on for several more minutes while the light became noticeably brighter. Gabriel's steps quickened and she felt his impatience to arrive at a place that was evidently important to him.

Out of the woods at last and before her stretched a ring of tall trees, their silver bark glinting in the sun. Boulders of white stone were scattered between slim trunks and within their strong guard a perfect circle of turf stretched as smooth as polished glass. A stillness pervaded the scene, a quietness, something almost holy. She felt she should speak in a whisper.

'Is this where you came as a boy?'

He looked at her, his face warmed by the soft light dusting the cloistered space. 'It is. Right here. It was our secret hideaway. Our tutor never found us, but then he was a portly fifty years and very scared of snakes!'

'And did you play in the magic circle?'

'We did. It was King Arthur's round table, or the deck of our pirate ship, or a clearing in the Amazon jungle. It was whatever we wanted it to be. One day we staged the entire Battle of Hastings, which was some feat with a cast of two. Of course, I was Harold – I was always on the losing side – and fell from the arrow in my eye round about there.' And he pointed to a shallow dip in the ground just short of the encircling trees.

She smiled to herself at the thought of two small boys playing day after day in this wonderful theatre, but Gabriel was no longer looking at the space that surrounded them. He seemed to be looking within. 'Sometimes,' he said slowly, 'we simply lay on its soft turf and watched the sky, whiling the hours away, daydreaming our futures.'

There was a long silence and Elinor knew instinctively not to speak. The very air seemed to crumble beneath the weight of his sadness. 'This is one future neither of us could have dreamed.'

But when she reached out tentatively to touch his arm, he said lightly enough, 'I trust, Mistress Nell, that with a secret place to visit, your love of Amersham will be greater than ever.'

She was unsure if she would ever dare the snakes alone, but beguiled that he had shared with her what seemed the happiest moments of his life. He jumped up from the fallen log and turned to head back the way they had come.

'We should return. I have to speak to Parsons and it must be time for you to find Martha.' His breezy tone blew away the last threads of intimacy.

His parting words were just as business-like. 'The fair is quite an occasion, you know. I hope you will go tomorrow. The servants are free to attend – you should make sure to enjoy yourself.'

Elinor was left to make a belated curtsy and slowly find her way back to the creamery. It had been a strange encounter, but Gabriel Claremont was home again and the knowledge warmed her.

Chapter Eight

As the duke promised every member of his staff was granted leave to attend the fair the following afternoon. Elinor had no real wish to go. She had seen plenty of such affairs and far more elaborate ones during her time in Bath, but neither did she relish being the sole servant left behind. Even the stately Mr Jarvis intended to be there. So she donned her laundered poplin and her only bonnet and sallied forth with her fellows. As soon as they arrived at the village green the party from Amersham Hall broke into smaller groups, men and maids going their separate ways to enjoy the merrymaking on offer. Sometimes going the same way, Elinor noted. She wished she could lead their uncomplicated lives.

A veritable cacophony of smells and noises greeted her as she stepped onto the green. The space had been parcelled out into a large number of booths and standings, many of which were crammed high with food. The stalls for oysters and sausages seemed particularly popular, but there were lines of gilt gingerbread and a number of hot pie sellers. Here and there tables and chairs had been set up for people to sit and eat their fill. There were stalls selling clothes and a number of toy displays for the children, gay with decorative paint and many coloured lamps.

But the predominant interest of the fair was entertainment. Elinor saw in the distance the Rector of Amersham, looking somewhat aghast, and wondered whether he had given his approval to such wholesale abandonment: horse riders doing tricks, tumblers, illusionists, even a knife swallower. In the background a band of itinerant musicians consisting of a double drum, a Dutch organ, a tambourine, violin and pipes was playing a selection of military tunes. She walked past food and toy stalls, past the fire eater who drew gasps from his captive crowd, past the puppet show that was clearly entrancing Tilly. On and on, never pausing until she was outside the tent of the fair's clairvoyant. Why ever had she had stopped here when she considered fortune telling thoroughly foolish?

It was dingy inside and the figure seated towards the back of the tent was wrapped in so many scarves of gauze that it was impossible to discern much of her features. Elinor wished she had not entered; it was a stupid thing to have done. But the figure's outstretched arm beckoned her to sit down, while a hand opened to receive the small coin Elinor had taken from her reticule.

'You have chosen well, my dear.' The voice was rasping as though it had travelled through layers of dusty parchment.

'I have?' She was nonplussed, having no idea what this strange creature was talking about.

'You have chosen well in visiting me. Of all those at the fair, I am the one you have chosen.'

How had the old woman known that? She must have

been watching me, Elinor guessed, watching me as I walked around the fairground. It was an uncomfortable thought.

The woman reached out again for both of Elinor's hands and turned them palms upwards. 'What do we have here, my dearie?' she croaked. 'Ah yes, I see an interesting future for you. There'll be a man for sure, a man to care for you and children to love. And they're coming soon.'

It was the old staple of fortune telling, she thought caustically. Tell any girl who comes your way she will shortly be married and she will leave happy. But the woman was tightening the pressure on her hands and bringing them closer to her veiled eyes.

Her voice had dwindled now to a hoarse whisper. 'You have chosen well in coming to Amersham.'

She must mean the village, Elinor thought, not the Hall, unless the crone had earlier seen her in company with those she knew to be its servants. Another wave of discomfort flooded through her. She had been comprehensively spied upon! Indignation urged her to rise and leave, but the woman's next words were confounding.

'Amersham Hall is your home.' It was a statement of fact which allowed no dissent.

'For the time being,' Elinor amended.

'Amersham Hall is your home, my dear. You have come home for good.'

She felt a shiver of recognition, but promptly dismissed it. True, she had felt a sense of belonging from the very first night, but her home? The grandest of houses belonging to a duke? It was nonsense.

'I'm not sure I know what you mean,' she said weakly.

The woman brushed across her palms again and fell slowly into a deep trance. Her eyes half-closed, she swayed slightly and her voice when it came was like the rush of wind before a storm.

'There is a woman. Dark hair. Skin as white as alabaster. She comes from over the sea, but she is in distress. Distress.' The syllables hissed around the hot enclosed space and Elinor felt her forehead break out in perspiration while a cold prickling flew down her spine.

'Her eyes are the green of a deep, deep ocean. Amazing eyes,' the old woman crooned. 'But she is in distress.'

Elinor hardly dared to breathe.

'You will save her. You will make all right.'

'How?' There was no answer from her informant. 'How?' she stuttered again.

At this the woman jerked upright and emitted a sigh that echoed around the tent, a sigh so heavy that it seemed dragged from the very earth beneath their feet. Elinor was transfixed and could not move. Gradually the woman's eyes cleared and all vestige of the trance vanished.

She smiled cunningly, assessing her customer with newly focused eyes. 'You'll be all right, dearie. A nice man and plenty of babies in store for you.'

It was the trite commonplace of fortune telling again and she realized the séance was over. Whatever the woman had seen, she saw it no more. Elinor pushed back her chair hard and it fell to the ground.

'A few falls before you get there though.' And the woman let out a high-pitched cackle. Elinor fled.

She rushed through the tent flap as though pursued

by a thousand demons and crashed straight into Roland Frant. He took a firm hold of her shoulders to steady her and peered into her face. 'Is that you, Nell? Whatever is the matter?'

'It's nothing, Mr Frant,' she murmured. 'Really it is nothing.' The last thing she wanted was to tell what she had just heard.

'But, my dear, you came through that doorway like a bullet from a gun. Whatever ails you?' Her spirits sank. He was not going to let her go easily. 'If you are in any trouble, maybe I can help,' he coaxed.

'I am not in trouble, but thank you for your concern. It is merely I found the fortune teller a little frightening.'

For the first time he looked up at the sign which hung high above the tent. 'Madame Demelza?' He tutted loudly. 'My cousin's hand is everywhere. There was a time when the Amersham Fair was wholesome enjoyment, but now every low criminal for miles around makes it their business to set up shop.'

'It was only a piece of fun, Mr Frant,' she protested.

'But your face told quite another story.' She had to acknowledge that he was right; she had been deeply scared.

'You know, Nell,' he said confidentially, 'you should not visit such people. They are charlatans and want nothing but your money. I hope you did not pay her.'

'Only a very little.'

He wagged his finger. 'Even a little is too much. And see the result – you have been thoroughly frightened by whatever nonsense she has told you. That is foolish, most foolish.'

He might speak truly but really he was the prosiest of bores and she was tired of his censure. 'I am sure you are right. But if you will excuse me now, I will look for my fellows and join them.'

'It may be best if I stay with you until you have regained your equilibrium. I am happy to act as your escort.'

'There is no need – I am perfectly restored. But thank you,' she added as she saw an expression of pique flit across his face. Before he could insist further, she slipped from his grasp and walked hurriedly away in the opposite direction.

The fair was turning into a very bad afternoon. The jarring noise and coarse smells were stretching her nerves thin and Roland Frant's persistence had left her drained. It had come too quickly after the unnerving encounter with the clairvoyant. She'd had to be rude before she could shake him off.

She sank down at one of the tables trying to gather her wits. What had the creature meant with her talk of a pale woman in distress? When she'd repeated that word, Elinor had felt a physical pain shoot through her. And now she was supposed to save this poor unfortunate. It was a daunting imposition. But had the old woman in fact meant anything? Had she simply been enjoying her power to disturb and the evident discomfort of her victim? That was the most likely explanation. She must not dwell any further on the words she'd heard, but shrug them off for the nonsense they were.

It was easier to say than do for they echoed constantly in her mind. She sat immobile for minutes on end while all around her the sounds of enjoyment seemed to come from a far-off country. She was in a fair way to succumbing completely to the blue devils when a familiar voice hailed her.

'The fair is supposed to be a merry event so why so sad, Mistress Nell?'

The duke stood before her, dressed in a close fitting coat of glistening blue superfine, his shapely legs encased in tight dove-grey pantaloons and a pair of dazzling hessians, their little gold tassels swinging jauntily from side to side. She had never seen him look so magnificent. Somewhere his valet must be dancing a jig; twice in a week Summers had conquered the carelessness of his noble employer.

She must have been staring rather too hard because he said, 'One has to dress to impress at these events, Nell.'

She pulled herself together. 'You will certainly do that, Your Grace. Your boot tassels alone could buy the whole of this fair.'

She hadn't meant her words to sound quite so disparaging, but he seemed not to notice. 'And what about you?'

'Me?'

'Where is your dress to impress?'

'Servants do not have such luxury,' she said primly.

'Now that is where you're wrong. I have just bid farewell to Mrs Lucas who is looking most becoming in a peach satin turban. So where is yours?'

'I do not possess one,' she said repressively.

'Not a turban perhaps, but a dress rich in colour. Any colour but grey! It is not a flattering hue, though you look most comely.'

She flushed with annoyance. He might be her employer,

he might have taken her a little into his confidence, but he had no right to judge her choice of dress.

'I do not wear grey to flatter myself, Your Grace, I wear it because it is eminently serviceable. And I *am* in service.' It was something he seemed prone to forget.

'I am aware, but you see I have brought you something which will improve matters immensely.' And from behind his back the duke brought forth a corsage of tiny pink roses nestling within a spray of lavender. The pale pink and mauve blooms chimed perfectly with her gown.

'Thank you, but I cannot accept such a gift,' she stammered.

'Why ever not? Such a small present – but one I guarantee that will lift your spirits.' He paused for a moment. 'Tell me, why are you so low?'

'I have a headache,' she extemporised.

He lifted two sceptical eyebrows. 'And...'

For some reason she found herself blurting out her experience in the clairvoyant's tent. 'And I am supposed to rescue this poor woman,' she finished. 'How on earth am I to do such a thing?'

He waited until she had ended her recital, but at this final wail he burst out laughing. 'Nell, you cannot honestly believe such nonsense!'

'But she was in a deep trance, I swear, and why would she say such things?'

'Simply to make an impact. The trance is mere acting – bad acting at that – and the cryptic words will ensure you go away seriously awed by her powers. You will say to your fellows that they, too, should go to Madame Demelza's tent and be frightened out of their wits.'

'I think she saw me with the other servants,' Elinor said slowly.

'Of course she did, and what a ready market they would prove. But you've disappointed. Instead of hastening to their side and spreading the word, you have been sitting here with a face as long as a fiddle.'

Her mood lightened. 'You may be right but she was still quite alarming.

'If she weren't, would you have entertained for a minute one word she said?'

She would not, of course, and recognising the truth of this, she relaxed into a smile.

'Now will you allow me?'

He held out his hand and raised her to her feet. His grip was warm and strong and she wanted very much for it to continue. But he bent towards her and before she knew what was happening, had pinned the flowers to the bodice of her dress and stepped back to admire his handiwork.

'As I thought, a perfect complement. Now even the grey dress you love so much can burst into bloom.'

She didn't love it, not at all, but its Quaker qualities had proved a powerful shield against the world, allowing her to go about her business unremarked. Until now. The brushing of his hand against her breast had made her pale skin flame, but she could not allow him to see her disturbance. 'Thank you, sir, it is most kind in you.'

His face held a strange expression. 'Kind? I don't think so. Irresistible? More than likely.'

Why was everyone talking in riddles this afternoon?

She wanted to demand an explanation, but he was her employer and his whims were not hers to question. They were still standing close together, Gabriel seeming unable to take his eyes from her, when she caught a glimpse of Roland Frant a short distance away, glaring fixedly at them. His expression was not pleasant. It would be wise, she thought, to disappear at this moment. She thanked the duke again, made a small curtsy, and began the walk back to Amersham Hall.

Chapter Nine

Gabriel whipped up his horses and swirled out of the fair in a pocket of dust. He was angry and the bays felt it, twitching and bucking in their shafts. He was angry with himself. He should have kept his distance and he hadn't. The dairymaid held a fascination for him he could not explain. He thought back to yesterday, back to the woods and the secret glade. He had not been there since returning from the Peninsular. He could not have borne to do so and yet a few hours ago he had gone willingly and shared it with a girl he hardly knew, a servant girl at that. Conduct verging on the imbecilic. But he'd felt at peace with Nell beside him. He had no idea why that should be and it made him uneasy. For nigh on two years he had not wanted to be close to anyone and after yesterday's unwise confidences, he'd drawn a silent line for himself which he'd vowed he would not again cross.

And what had he just done? He'd presented her with a corsage for her dress. Flowers, for heaven's sake! He'd seen her sitting quite alone amongst a crowd of people, her eyes lowered, her shoulders sad. A little, grey mouse. No, a tall, grey mouse. And he'd wanted to brighten her, to lighten her, to light up her eyes. The roses had been to hand and he hadn't thought twice. He should have done. It was beyond stupid to single out one servant for special treatment, and this servant in particular.

He was still suspicious, convinced there was something smoky about her and that was an added reason, if he needed one, to keep away. He knew nothing of her references, but presumed they were satisfactory. That was a matter for Jarvis and the butler seemed happy enough. Still, she had to be something more than the simple servant she claimed. Her manners, her voice, her education all told a different tale.

Whatever her history, he seemed impelled to gravitate towards her and it could not continue. He must put her back where she belonged – in the dairy and at arms' length. Within the next few days his house guests would bring their interminable stay to an end and he would go with them back to Brighton, to the colour and intemperance of that lively town. That should do the trick. There was nothing to keep him here since Joffey, despite his faults, was capable of managing the estate without assistance. Jonathan would have done it differently, he knew; Jonathan would have flourished as the master of Amersham.

He remembered their childhood games when they had fashioned crowns from cardboard and robes from old curtains. Jonty had always claimed the larger crown and the richer material and he had been content to let him. In his childish way he'd recognised Jonathan was the important one, that one day his brother would be this person called a duke and that it was right he should practice. The practice never lasted more than a few minutes, just until one of them tripped and fell on the over-long gown, a speedy invitation for the other to leap in and start an almighty tussle. The skirmish ended only when two small boys became inextricably trussed in the folds of curtain and were rolled tight together, side by side, like sausages in a pan.

But Jonathan was dead and he had survived. Except for a quirk of military strategy he should have been one of the five thousand slain on the battlefield of Vitoria. While his brother lay dying, he was pinned the other side of rugged mountains with only a narrow defile to allow a straggle of troops to reach the plain below. Jonathan had died alone and far from Amersham. His remains had been scooped up and lowered into a hasty grave – the heat of a Spanish summer made rapid burial essential. The war was over and the grave lost. Jonty would never come home.

For his brother's sake he had tried to play the duke, but his heart wasn't in it. He needed to be elsewhere. He would return to Brighton, a town where masquerade was woven into the very texture of the air, and he would plunge into every last one of its dissipations. Until then he would keep out of Nell Milford's way and this time really mean it. His guests, with one accord, had shunned this afternoon's fair, complaining bitterly at his own forced attendance. Tomorrow he would offer them compensation – a cross-country ride with a picnic as its goal. The outing would do double duty, ensuring his day was spent far from the Hall and far from temptation.

⌒

Elinor awoke the next morning still unsettled by events

at the fair. In particular the clairvoyant loomed large in her mind and, though she knew the duke was right when he said cryptic utterances were vital to the old woman's business, she couldn't quite shake off the idea that some of it had meaning. The duke hadn't been in the tent; hadn't heard the change in the woman's voice from platitude to urgency; hadn't seen her frighteningly blank face when she'd dropped into a trance. And afterwards he'd done little to make her feel more comfortable. Had made things worse in fact. Why accost her and then pin flowers to her breast? She had them still, brightening the small room she shared with Tilly. Last night the kitchen maid had teased her to distraction, mocking her for her unknown admirer. What would she say if she knew the flowers had come from the Duke of Amersham himself?

It was a fantasy, though, to imagine his actions were anything more than a whim and she was in danger of drifting, charmed by the beauty of Amersham and charmed by its owner: the moments when they'd met and talked, the times when they'd crossed swords, the walk she had taken with him, the flowers she would keep pressed in her private notebook. She hadn't felt so alive for years, but she must not allow herself to sit out the summer in a dream. She must take action and soon.

She found Martha already at work. The woman looked up briefly and gave a grunt. 'Get ter work on the cream, Nell. It needs be ready by ten.'

'Ten! But Cook -'

'Nuthing to do with Cook. The nobs is on a picnic and leaving around eleven.'

Elinor's ears pricked, wondering if this might be her chance. 'Do you know where they intend to picnic?'

Her mentor was evidently ruffled at having her schedule torn to pieces and her tone was truculent. 'All I knows is the carridge taking the food leaves at ten and there'll be 'ell to pay if we ain't ready fer it.'

Elinor thought better of prolonging the conversation and set to work as fast as she could. By five minutes to the hour they had filled sufficient boxes with butter, cream and cheese.

'Yer best get it to the 'ouse, I'll clean up 'ere. Leastways they'll be gorn all day, if we're lucky,' the older woman muttered testily.

This was sounding promising. If the company rode out and the duke rode with them, it might at last provide the opportunity to search Gabriel's study undisturbed. She resolved she would take the chance. It was likely to be the only one she would get.

On the stroke of ten she delivered their handiwork to the kitchen and for a while stood quietly listening to her fellow servants. They were in high spirits and ready to talk, knowing they would be free of ringing bells for at least four hours. Only two ladies were staying behind and they had ordered refreshments to be taken to the small front parlour. They were on their way there now, armed with copies of *La Belle Assemblée*. Tea and chatter would keep them company. The parlour was situated at the very end of one of the building's wings and therefore as distant from the study as Elinor could hope.

~

It was well before noon when she heard the crunch of horses on gravel as a large body of riders made its way to the main gate. She had been scrubbing the ironwork tables and chairs on the small terrace outside the dairy and listened intently as the sound of hooves gradually faded. She forced herself to wait for several minutes before stepping inside, her pulse beginning to tumble at the thought of what she was about to do.

'Martha, I forgot to mention that while I was at the house, Cook asked me to deliver the rest of today's cream this morning.'

Martha looked nonplussed. 'But she don't like it till near dinner time. Else it goes orf.'

'She surprised me too,' she lied glibly, 'but she was quite adamant. I believe she is trying out a new kind of dessert and the cream has to be mixed in at an early stage.'

The older woman shrugged her bony shoulders irritably. 'If yer must go, but don't be long.'

Elinor snatched up the two containers they had recently filled and almost ran out of the dairy. She had no idea what Cook would say when presented with cream far in advance of her needs, but hopefully by then she would be out of earshot. She dropped the cream into the kitchen, making sure it was not easily visible, and then found the small passage she had wandered into by mistake on her second evening at Amersham. In a minute she was in the stone-flagged Great Hall. A temporary hush had descended on the house as it did every day at this time. Half the servants' work had been done and there was a brief rest before they began again on the hours of toil that still awaited them. She darted across the hall, deliberately avoiding the beak-like stares of Gabriel's ancestors, and carefully tried the door to the study. The handle turned easily. Slipping inside, she closed the door very, very quietly. The room faced towards the rear of the house looking out on a vista of rolling lawns, a lake with a fountain at its centre and to the right, a well-tended rose garden. Beyond the Capability Brown inspired hills and hollows stretched pasture land and grazing cattle. Of human beings there was not a sign.

She would have to work fast, but this time she was unencumbered by candlelight, the sun shining broadly through large casements and illuminating every corner of the room. A couple of mahogany cabinets were positioned against one wall while a modest bookcase took up another. There were several small tables and a scattering of easy chairs. She was surprised to think this was Gabriel's study. It was a room devoid of his presence, a room from which all personality had fled. It was also disconcertingly tidy and if there were papers here, they had been stored well out of sight. The cabinets offered an invitation, but there was one other piece of furniture that dominated the room: a large desk that sat in the window enclave and looked outwards to the demesne beyond. This was where she would start.

She was in luck. The drawers were unlocked. She opened them one by one and skimmed their contents: discarded pens, old envelopes, several visiting cards and a few crumpled bills which appeared to have lain there for ever. Nothing of any interest. One drawer left, positioned at the side of the desk rather than the front, and it appeared to be locked. She felt a rising excitement. She had seen a key in the first drawer she'd opened and with fumbling hands fitted it to the lock. It turned easily. That cannot be right, she thought. And it wasn't. The drawer was completely empty and why it had been locked was a mystery.

A hurried glance around. Should she move on to the mahogany cabinets? But no, she was sure this desk held the clues she sought although she could not see how. She tipped out the contents of the pen container but all she found was a collection of battered quills. She turned the blotter upside down but it remained disappointingly intact. She felt beneath the desk rim for a possible secret drawer. Not a creak or a grind of hinges. Disgusted, she was about to give up on the desk and begin on the rest of the room when her foot accidentally caught in one of its carved legs. There was a sharp click and a small compartment shot out from inside of the desk's writing surface, from what she had taken to be a simple leather inlay.

Her face grew pink with anticipation. There *was* a secret drawer! Might there also be secret papers? But when she wrenched the compartment out to its fullest extent, not a scrap was to be seen. Urgently she jiggled the drawer and was answered by a slight metallic sound. A golden object, curled into a small heap, slid to the front of the drawer. She drew it out almost reverently and laid it on her palm. Her heart almost stopped as she realised what she was staring at – a locket or rather one half of a locket on a broken chain, and inside a beautifully executed miniature of a young man, fresh faced and blue eyed. She studied the face intently, looked and looked again, as though by sheer looking she could draw out his very spirit and urge him to speak. It was the mirror image of the broken locket she carried on her person. But how could that be? The soft movement of a door sounded behind her, but so caught up was she in the confusing whirl of thoughts that she heard nothing.

Chapter Ten

A voice sliced through the air. 'And what *precisely* do you think you're doing?'

Gabriel stood in the doorway, his riding dress muddied and torn, his whip still in his hand. She whirled around, her back shielding the nakedness of the open drawer and her hand closing over the locket.

'Mrs Lucas asked me to deliver a message,' she improvised.

'And since when has my housekeeper found it necessary to employ a dairymaid as messenger?'

She was struck dumb. 'You are silent. Now why is that?' All trace of geniality had vanished and she felt her soul wither. 'But let us presume for one moment that Mrs Lucas has been so unseemly as to send you here – where is the message?'

Her mind was ragged. Bewildered by what she had found, she needed time to think. In desperation she cast around for a new pretext, but before she could find the words, he had raised his hand to silence her.

'Spare me the lies, Nell! I have continued to trust you despite your questionable conduct, but I can see that I have been mistaken. Today I find you in my private room, your hands in my desk, a blatant trespasser once more.'

His chill glance swept her figure and unnervingly came to rest on the tell-tale closed hand. 'And a thief, it seems.'

He was standing so close that she could see every fleeting emotion and his expression did not bode well. He tugged her hand open and the miniature fell to the ground. As he bent to scoop the locket from the floor, she saw his brow furrow.

'I trust you have a valid reason for stealing my jewellery.' His voice was the thinnest and sharpest of steel. 'You had better explain yourself – and start now!'

Elinor felt anger flicker within her and slowly gather pace. She had been right to think there was a mystery attached to Amersham. The matching lockets proved that. The truth, whatever it was, had meaning for her but it had been deliberately hidden. She drew herself up to her full height and when she spoke her voice was as cold as his. 'It is you, Your Grace, who needs to explain. How has this miniature come into your possession?'

'What the devil! Why should it not be in my possession? You found it in *my* study, in *my* desk, and it is an image of *my* uncle.'

'Your uncle?' she faltered, her certainty deserting her. The miniature bore so little resemblance to the forbidding portrait in the Great Hall that she had felt not a flicker of recognition.

'What has that to say to anything?'

'I don't know, I don't understand.'

'You are not alone. What I do understand is that you

are unruly, disobedient and guilty of the most brazen transgression. If you stay in my employ, which I doubt, you will be punished severely. Now leave.'

'I cannot, Your Grace. Not until I know. You have been withholding a secret that matters dearly to me. Why have you not been honest?'

'What the deuce are you talking about?' The arctic glare had been replaced by an irritated frown.

'I cannot believe you had no knowledge of this locket and no understanding of its significance. In your own words – tell me the truth and spare me the lies.'

'Is this to be a Banbury story? Speak plainly and be warned that those who set out to gull me have a habit of coming off very much the worst.' The glare was back, but Elinor knew no fear.

'I am convinced the half locket in your hand holds the clue to my mother's past and perhaps to my own identity.'

'What nonsense is this? What connection can there be between an image of my uncle and a dairymaid?'

'I am no dairymaid.'

'You're certainly no dairymaid that I've ever come across.'

His natural good humour was beginning to undermine his wrath. Then he remembered her crime. 'If you think to bamboozle me with this silly tale straight out of a romance – oh, but you don't read them do you? If you think to hoodwink me, you will not succeed. I have never seen this miniature before and even if I had, what has it to do with you?'

In answer she drew one half of a gold locket and chain

from the depths of her pocket and placed it on the desk. 'I think it has much to do with me. See, Your Grace, I have the matching portrait.'

He gazed at the beautiful young woman depicted. The miniature was intricately wrought and faithful in every detail. It was an answering image of the locket Elinor had taken from the desk. He looked up. The cloud of dark hair and the misty green eyes of the painting were right there before him.

'Who is this and why do you have it?' She knew he must already have the answer.

'It is a picture of my mother and is the sole remembrance I have of her.' And suddenly the fortune teller's words came flooding back. This was the woman she had been describing, the woman from over the sea, the woman Elinor was to save. Her own mother!

'Your mother? What has she to do with this?'

'She was a painter and specialised in miniatures. I believe she painted this image of herself and the one of your uncle.'

'Then your mother was commissioned by my Uncle Charles? Is that what you're saying?'

She smiled at his simplicity. 'Not exactly. The two halves of the locket belong together – see here.' And she slotted the small hinges one into the other without hindrance. 'The strands of each chain fit together, too.'

He was frowning even harder, but she continued, 'These are matching portraits. I think they must have been painted by one lover for another.'

'That is ridiculous. What you're suggesting is insane.

My uncle's wife was a Louisa Lovejoy and she stills lives. More's the pity.'

So there was no death or divorce, Elinor thought, remembering the fiercely scratched out name in the family Bible. But a repudiation, a banishment? 'I wasn't talking about marriage,' she managed with difficulty.

'An affair?' He was nothing if not candid. 'Uncle Charles was whiter than white, but even if he *had* enjoyed a youthful dalliance with a stray artist, what has it to do with you?'

His description of her mother hurt, but she was too flustered to respond. The duke had hit on the very question she was struggling to answer.

'There was a scandal, I believe,' she said falteringly. 'A scandal that involved my mother. My father, too, perhaps.'

'You divine all this from a broken locket?'

Elinor refused to be deflected. 'On her deathbed my mother urged me to come here. Why would she do so, if she had no connection to this place?'

'You were to come *here*?'

'To Amersham,' she said firmly. 'And seek out one who would help me, one who was rich and powerful. That could only be your uncle.'

He stared blankly at her and she pushed her advantage. 'He is the one my mother spoke of. He has to be. Eighteen years ago he was the only young man living here. The family Bible makes that clear.'

'So that was the reason you were poking and prying in the library,' he said bullishly. 'And I was almost taken in by Cicero!'

'I had to know why my mother was so desperate for me

to come to Amersham. I owed it to her.'

'All you know,' he said flatly, 'is that at some time in the past your mother painted my uncle.'

'You have forgotten the nature of the portraits. They are painted in matching style and form two halves of a complete locket. It is the kind of object lovers exchange with each other. The locket has not been broken, you can see, but deliberately sundered, so that each lover might keep a remembrance of their sweetheart.'

'But that's nonsense. If what you say were true, why would they keep their own portrait?' He sounded triumphant.

'All I can think is that it was too dangerous for them to possess an image of their lover. It had to be enough to know they shared the same locket.'

A look of derision crossed his face. 'Most affecting but highly unlikely. It is pure speculation, in fact wild speculation. Tell me this, if there had been such a love affair, where does your father fit in?'

'I have no idea,' she said miserably. 'I cannot even tell you his name.'

The duke gaped. 'You do not know your father's name?'

'My mother would never speak of him. She was adamant I need never know. All I learned was that she arrived in Bath alone and that I was born months later.'

He was shaking his head in disbelief, but Elinor would not let the moment slip. 'Please help me, Your Grace, help me uncover the past.'

'I cannot imagine why you think to do so here.'

'Somewhere in this great sprawl of a mansion, there must be papers – your uncle's personal papers – and they might shed light on what happened all those years ago. They might even tell me if I have a father living.'

She could see her words had hit home. After some minutes he said slowly, 'I accept this is a matter of great import to you and because of that, I am willing to forget your trespass. But what you ask is impossible.'

'Why impossible? Is it that you do not believe my mother and your uncle were lovers?'

'It matters not what I believe. There may even be some truth in what you say. As a child I seem to recall some kind of scandal being whispered about. But I never knew the details and we are unlikely to discover them at this remove.'

'It is surely worth trying. For all my nineteen years I have been left ignorant of my true history.'

A tear was slowly making its way down one pale cheek and despite his disbelief, Gabriel could not remain indifferent.

'Do you not think,' he said gently, 'that if there were such secrets as you suggest, they would have been well and truly swept beneath the carpet. There will be nothing to find.'

'I must try.'

'And if there is nothing?'

'Then I must accept I will never know the truth.'

He began to pace up and down the study floor as though continual movement would clear the mists clouding his mind.

A disapproving tut brought him to a halt. He glared at her. 'What?'

'Your feet. You are making the carpet filthy and it will

take the housemaid hours to clean it.'

'Forgive me. For the moment I had forgot you are one of my servants,' he said acidly.

'Why are you home at this time?'

He looked at her in astonishment. A moment ago she had been threatened with instant dismissal, yet here she was daring to challenge him. Anger battled with laughter and laughter won. 'Nell Milford, you are incorrigible.'

'And...'

'And my horse is lame. I should not have taken her out. I thought there was a problem yesterday, but I ignored it in my arrogant, aristocratic way. I was forced to turn back at the second field. Unluckily for you.'

'Luckily for me. You are going to help, aren't you?'

He looked at the lovely young face so close to his and capitulated. 'Where are we supposed to start this ridiculous search of yours?'

'Your Uncle Charles must have kept records that were personal to him.'

'He might have done. I have no idea.'

'His death was sudden, I believe,' she said thoughtfully, 'so he would not have had the chance to destroy sensitive papers.'

'If there were any such, Joffey would have seen to them after my uncle's funeral. I found nothing in this room.'

'The bailiff would not have destroyed them, not without permission.' Her voice had become certain. 'So where could he have stored them?'

'The cellars most like. There's a large storeroom next to the winery and Charles had his own key to it. God knows what's in there, apart from the rats, that is.'

He saw her shudder. 'Not so brave now? Want to give up the whole foolish project?'

'No.' Her voice was unwavering. 'I haven't travelled this far to be deterred by a few rats.'

'Not even an army of them? Big, fat, sleek rats running and diving and nipping where they like.'

She was laughing now, but her face was alight with excitement. 'Not even an army of them.'

'If you're that committed, we had better do it. But I don't want anyone else to know. I have no intention of creating a fuss for no reason and I certainly don't wish to be caught in the cellar with my dairymaid! If this is all a hum – and I'm sure it is – the fewer people that know about it the better. Is that clear?'

'Yes, Your Grace,' she agreed meekly.

'My guests leave in the morning. I was to travel with them, but I shall invent some excuse. Once the household is abed tomorrow night, we will make a search. Wrap up warmly, the cellars are cold even in June.'

'There will be just the two of us?'

'Who else were you thinking of inviting to this charade?' She had no answer and he repeated with some enjoyment, 'Just the two of us.'

'And is it really necessary that we search at night?'

'Why, whatever is the matter, Mistress Nell? You can brave the rats, but not me?'

Her chin jutted determinedly. 'I will be there.'

Chapter Eleven

This night of all nights Tilly took an age to fall asleep. Once her head hit the pillow she could usually be relied upon to snore the next seven hours away, but tonight for some inexplicable reason groans rather than snores filled the room and her constant tossing and turning was sending her covers flying to the floor. Nerves taut, Elinor lay still and silent on the adjoining bed, listening to the kitchen maid's disturbed threshing. Listening, listening for the elusive noise which would signal Tilly at last slept.

It was gone midnight before she could creep from the room. She was fully dressed beneath her nightgown and, slipping the garment over her head, she grabbed her unlit candle and inched her way round the door. Once outside she paused for a second, but Tilly's regular heavy breathing was the only sound she could hear. She fled down the servants' staircase, wondering if her journey was in vain since Gabriel had expected her hours ago. The servants rarely stayed up beyond eleven o'clock and by now he might well have given her up. It was annoying that he would think her too scared to face either him or the rats, but it was also a grievous setback to her quest. The clairvoyant's words had given her new impetus. She owed it to her mother as much as to herself to uncover whatever secret history lay within the bones of Amersham.

When she reached the cellar, she felt huge relief at finding him still there. In the flickering candlelight she could see he wore a grim expression and when he spoke his voice was edged with impatience.

'Where have you been? You've kept me waiting for well over an hour.'

'I am sorry to have delayed you,' she said with the slightest hint of tartness, 'but I could do no other. Tilly has only just gone to sleep.'

'Tilly? Who the...Who is Tilly?'

'The kitchen maid who shares my room.'

He looked surprised at the information, as well he might. His world and hers were poles apart and she wondered if he had any idea how his servants lived.

'Now you *are* here, let's get on with it.'

He had already unlocked the massive oak door which faced them, its surface patterned with cruel iron spikes. It was a door which clearly said Keep Out, but not to the Duke of Amersham. He pointed to its huge, rusty lock. 'The key took an age to locate so this better be worth the effort.'

The cellar appeared to Elinor to be larger than most people's dwellings and a great deal dirtier. Household items discarded over centuries marched along each wall. At intervals stacks of files and loose documents lurched in drunken columns, with one or two having given up all hope of ever staying upright and scattering themselves profligately across the floor. Her eyes glanced from one pile to another and her spirits sank.

'Where do you wish to start, Miss Milford?'

There was a trace of glee in his voice. He was enjoying her discomfiture, hoping no doubt she would turn tail and give up. She was not going to.

As her eyes gradually adjusted to the dim light, detail began to emerge, and even in the gloomy haze she could plainly see that the rats had enjoyed their sojourn. Virtually every stack of documents had been set upon by sharp little teeth and now much of what had doubtless been priceless history was nothing more than dust. She bent down to peer at the column of papers nearest her. Unusually it had been left almost whole by the rats and riffling its surface she found a medley of tailor's bills, invoices from gun merchants, hastily jotted notes and a stack of letters, some torn into scraps. She looked more closely and part of a faded signature caught her eye.

'This is where we'll start,' she said coolly.

He shrugged his shoulders and squatted down on the floor and in a few moments she had joined him. She allowed herself a quiet smile. If the cellar had a window, protocol would be vanishing through it right now. The first documents they turned over were of relatively recent date and could be quickly discarded. But they gave her hope since Charles' personal papers appeared to have been moved by Joffey *en masse*. There must be a chance they would uncover documents from that crucial time when her mother – and she felt certain of this – had fled the district for Bath.

They moved on through bundle after bundle of papers,

the years gradually passing by their blurred vision. As the dates grew older, they began to move more cautiously. It was a slow process. Year might follow year but the documents were a confused mix of letters, memos, notes, bills, even doodles, and each sheet had to be carefully perused. Somewhere in the house a clock struck two. She was bemused at hearing its chimes. Could it really be two whole hours that she had been kneeling here? Her dress was grimy and her eyes red with soreness.

'This is ridiculous.' Gabriel's voice echoed off the walls. 'I'm a peer of the realm. I command half the county and most of its population. And here I am, filthy and tired, looking for I don't know what. You're a witch, Nell Milford.'

She looked astonished.

'Yes, a witch. To entice me down to this hell hole for no good reason.' He heaved a sigh which seemed to come from the bottom of his now sadly scuffed hessians. 'There's just one more batch ...' and he flicked through the remaining huddle of papers that were still intact, '...they appear to start around 1795 – but if we find nothing, the matter is closed. You will never mention it again. Is that understood?'

She nodded in agreement, but had already begun to sift through the papers. Two thirds of the way down this last bundle, she struck what she thought was gold. It was a letter from a John Fortescue of Warwick Court, the City of London. Its bold, black heading made clear that John Fortescue was an enquiry agent. The letter was brief and to the point. After the customary salutation and several pious wishes for the then marquis's good health, it concluded:

I have searched the entire county of Sussex, so too the adjoining counties, and though I have expended the greatest of diligence, I regret that I have been unable to trace the person your lordship has been most anxious to find.

Who had he been looking for? She caught her breath. Surely it had to be her mother. The young Charles Claremont had been looking for Grainne, but had been unable to find her. The agent had not searched widely enough. One more county and he might have discovered his quarry in Bath.

'Look,' she said, her hand trembling as she held the letter out to the duke. The candlelight etched deep lines on his face and his response was equally uncompromising. 'This tells us nothing.'

'But it does, surely it does. Your uncle was looking for his lover, but failed to find her.'

'You have a lively imagination. He could have been looking for anyone.'

'But who else would he wish to find so urgently? And why would he employ an enquiry agent from London? Choosing such a man indicates the search was very important and one that had to be conducted in the greatest of secrecy.'

'Even if that were true, the letter itself proves nothing,' he said flatly. 'I'm sorry, Nell, but as evidence it's as tenuous as the locket.'

She bowed her head. He was right, of course. She had stopped thinking sensibly. She was tired, so tired she could hardly keep herself upright. Her eyelids drooped, her body slackened and she had almost toppled to the floor when she felt strong, steady arms around her. It felt good, safe almost. She must be mad. She was in the most dangerous of places and with a most dangerous man. His face was very close and she could feel the warmth of his skin next to hers. She had only to stretch out her hand and she could run her fingers down the strong cheek bones until she reached a mouth which was full and warm and inviting. What was she thinking? She moved rapidly back from him and in doing so, caught the glimpse of a knowing smile.

But when he spoke, his voice gave nothing away. 'You are weary and you must work tomorrow. Go to bed. I will check what documents are left and if, as I suspect, I find nothing, you must accept you have been mistaken.'

She began to get to her feet and in her fatigue knocked against a stash of old hunting rifles that had been propped against the cellar wall. They fell to the floor with a deafening clang. She stood immobile waiting for the reverberations to cease, terrified the noise was loud enough to bring others to the scene. If so, how could she ever explain this night time rendezvous? No one would believe such a far-fetched story as she had to tell. But nothing stirred above and she slowly allowed her breath to escape. The guns had dislodged an old hunting bag, dusty brown leather but of evident good quality with tooled flaps and solid brass buckles and clasp.

'These weapons should have been got rid of years ago,' Gabriel complained. 'By now they must be positively unsafe.'

'Whose were they?' she asked, though she was too dispirited really to wish to know.

'They belonged to Charles. Hunting was a passion with him.'

'And the bag?'

'His too. This stuff must have been here for years.'

'From when he was a young man?'

'Probably. The guns are very old-fashioned. He would have replaced them with something a good deal smarter. He never spared money on hunting equipment.'

She picked up the bag and several old shotgun shells fell to the floor. 'He doesn't seem to have been very careful. Look at this ammunition he's left lying around.'

'It's almost certainly corrupted.' Gabriel had risen to his feet and was gathering together the scattered shotguns.

'This one certainly is.' She had picked up a battered shell and shook it. A grey cloud of ash poured forth, interspersed with slivers of white which looked almost like paper. She looked again. It was paper! These were fragments of burnt paper! She picked up another of the spent shells and shook it fiercely. The same result.

'These empty cartridges – someone has attempted to destroy papers and then hide the evidence inside,' she said excitedly.

'Not just attempted. They pretty much succeeded.' Gabriel's foot traced a swirl in the fallen ash.

'It must have been Charles.'

'And what if it were? What possible use can a heap of ash be?'

'I don't know,' she said a trifle mournfully, 'except to show he had something to hide and was paranoid about secrecy. Otherwise he would have burnt the papers in a grate and left the ashes there.'

She picked up the last shell. A larger sliver of white appeared at its edge and intrigued, she picked at it with her fingernail. Slowly she manoeuvred her find from inside the shell case and then unwound the spiral of paper that emerged. It was the smallest fragment of a page, its edges a curled brown, but some of the ink marks had survived and were just about decipherable.

She grabbed what was left of both candles and peered at the writing which scrawled itself across the page. Her hands were shaking.

'Look!'

'I'd like to,' he said acidly. 'What exactly am I looking at?'

'There are a few words only, but is that your uncle's writing?' She handed him the fragment and willed him to agree.

'It's his writing all right.'

'We have found something,' she almost shrieked.

'I know we are fifteen feet below the rest of the household, but keep your voice down. I cannot afford for my staff to discover me in such compromising circumstances. Think what it would do to my reputation!'

The pleasantry went over her head. 'It has come from a journal,' she said eagerly, 'a very personal journal, I'm sure. He must have destroyed the rest.' They glanced at the ash beneath their feet.

'I think I can see why.' Gabriel's face was unusually forbidding. 'The first few words are clear enough. G... *with child*...then there's *what have we* and the word after that looks like *done*. There's a ...*must* and a *Louisa*. The last line is badly burnt but I'm sure it says... yes, it says, *no hope*.'

Elinor listened to the words and crumpled. The shock had rendered her limbs useless. She had imagined the duke and her mother lovers, imagined a scandal and perhaps a hasty departure, even that her father had turned his face from his wife, but not this.

'She was carrying your uncle's child!'

Gabriel looked stunned. 'He was such a martinet of a man!' he blurted out. 'It is almost impossible to believe – your mother with child, and by him.' He walked up and down almost in a trance. Then he burst out, 'And you were the child. You had to be.' He fingered again the fragment of burnt paper. 'There's no date here, but it has to be you. Your mother had no other child and neither did he.'

She looked at him dazedly. 'I am his daughter?' There were long moments of silence. 'But what of my own father?' She paused. 'Or the man I thought to be my father.'

'What indeed. It would seem he never existed. You have no name, no direction, nothing that suggests he was anything more than an idea. And there is no one on the estate who could tell us for certain – even Jarvis came here a few years after my uncle's marriage – but I would bet that your mother never married, that there was no husband. No wonder she kept silent.'

Elinor's face was a study of sadness. 'Why could your uncle not have married her?'

'Isn't it obvious? The family would never have accepted such an alliance.'

'Because my mother was a social inferior? She came

from a noble family in Ireland, or so I've been told.'

'An aristocrat earning her living as a painter?'

'She fled her home at a young age and used what skill she had to keep a roof over her head.'

'That scandal alone would have ensured my grandfather would never have countenanced the match – he would have been alive at the time – particularly when his younger son had muddied the family waters by eloping.'

'Your parents eloped?'

'They did and paid the price for the rest of their short lives. But in any case I believe Charles was betrothed to the unlovely Louisa when barely out of his teens. My grandfather would never have allowed him to break the contract.'

For a minute she was lost in thought. 'I see...that's what Charles meant. The *must* and *Louisa*. He was confiding to his diary that he had to marry Louisa, but he loved my mother.' She scrambled to her feet. 'There seems to have been little genuine love in your family.'

'There wasn't,' he said shortly. 'So where does all this leave us? Minus a dairymaid at Amersham, I would hazard.'

She looked confused and his voice softened. 'You will hardly wish to continue working in the dairy after the revelations of this night.'

'No, I suppose not. I haven't thought.' She was stammering a little. 'I will leave, of course, but only when it's convenient. I am happy to remain until Mr Jarvis has secured a replacement for me.'

'And what does that prim little speech mean?' He had taken up a familiar pose, leaning negligently against the cellar wall.

'It means that *when* I leave hardly matters. It's what I've discovered that is important. My journey has ended in a way I could never have imagined.'

'And how did you think it would end?' He sounded intrigued.

'I am not telling you.' Elinor felt very stupid.

'But you must. I need to know how much we have fallen short of your dream.'

She swallowed hard. 'I believed my mother was sending me to a man who had once befriended her and that perhaps he was elderly or a recluse or both, since as far as I knew they had not communicated for years.'

'An elderly recluse?' He hooted with laughter until she shushed him urgently, but he was not going to let the topic go. 'Tell me, why ever would you wish to visit such a one?'

'I didn't wish it. My mother made me promise. When she died, I lost the small income that afforded us food and shelter. She could see that this would happen and feared for my future. I think she hoped that Amersham would offer me a new security. I came because I had no choice. I hoped that I might be of use, that an elderly man might be glad of young company. Even, perhaps, that I could make my home here.'

She was feeling sillier than ever, but to her surprise Gabriel grabbed her hand and pressed it tightly. 'You were right about that at least. I hope you will make your home at Amersham.'

She shook her head vigorously. 'I cannot do that.'

'You must. It will be some small recompense.'

'I have my recompense. You helped me find it tonight.'

'That is hardly sufficient. My uncle was a villain to seduce a young woman and leave her to her fate.'

'He tried to find her,' she protested, surprised at his vehemence.

'But not very hard. He should have had the courage to face up to his father and refuse to marry where he was told, but instead he chose the cowardly path.'

'Can you truly blame him? Your grandfather sounds a tyrant.'

'Tyrant or not, my uncle's actions make him a blackguard.' The duke's tone was unequivocal.

'Yet my mother painted him with love.' He shrugged his shoulders impatiently. Any mention of love appeared to irritate him.

'We will talk later,' he said, ushering her from the cellar. 'Right now we must go from here before the household wakes.'

Chapter Twelve

Dawn was breaking as she clambered wearily up the stairs to her room. She had found some of the missing pieces to the jigsaw that was her mother's history. Incredible as it seemed, she appeared to be the illegitimate daughter of Charles Claremont, the 4th Duke of Amersham. She felt delirious from lack of sleep, but also deeply sad. The pain her mother had suffered in giving up the man she loved, to a woman for whom he cared nothing, must have been unbounded and made worse by the thorny path she had chosen to walk thereafter. No wonder she had never married despite her many Bath admirers. It was not because she loved a dead husband too fiercely, but because she loved a living, breathing man too much.

And where did this new knowledge leave her daughter? A heaviness descended on Elinor as she contemplated her future, confusing the excitement she'd felt only minutes ago. It was impossible to continue as a dairymaid, but equally impossible to make her home at Amersham as the duke had suggested. It was kind of him, but if she were foolish enough to agree he would be forced to acknowledge her birth. And what shame that would produce for the family, what gossip there would be in the county.

~

Gabriel spent what was left of the night pacing his bedroom floor. How could a secret such as this have been kept for so long? His own father must have known. He surely could not have been unaware of such momentous events in his brother's life. But if he had known, that knowledge had died with him in Jamaica. So who else could have known? Charles' wife? Never. His father? It was clear Charles had not braved that patriarch's wrath. He'd made a half-hearted attempt to find his lover, and having failed, buried their secret for ever. No doubt he'd burnt every incriminating document he could find, yet he had kept the locket which most clearly revealed his guilt. It seemed that in the end he could not bring himself to destroy the image painted by his lover. Perhaps Elinor was right in thinking them true sweethearts. Gabriel shook his head. That was mawkish and, to his way of thinking, simply proved once again how disastrous love could be.

The discoveries of the night had left him with a monumental problem – what to do with Elinor. She was almost certainly a cousin. An illegitimate one it was true, but still his relative and he could not allow her to be cast into poverty nor to continue making his butter and cheese. She would have to live here in the house, he decided, and he would have to hire a chaperon. He must delay a little longer going to Brighton; everything must be done properly. It was clear that both she and her mother had suffered deeply and he did not want to make things worse by exposing her to loose gossip. He would consult his aunt on how best to go about things. Roland was an idiot, despicable too, but his mother was a hard-headed woman whose pride in the Claremonts was second to none. She would know how to negotiate this tricky situation with the least scandal, and as a woman she could advise the best way to deal with a vulnerable girl.

He would need to remember that vulnerability for he had been tempted tonight, badly tempted. He had felt her within an inch of reaching out to him and his body had taken light. But thank God, he had stayed his hand. He could not use her so, and now he knew of their relationship, he must be ever more scrupulous in walking the right side of the line. The search for a chaperon was urgent.

An idea hit him in a blaze. It was simple but obvious – he would not hire a chaperon, he would persuade his aunt to take Elinor completely under her wing. The girl could live at the Dower House until her future was arranged. It was a clever solution. He would go to see his aunt tomorrow.

'Yer wanted up at the 'ouse.' Martha jerked a worn thumb in the direction of the sprawling pile.

'Do you know why?'

It was a foolish question, but Elinor was apprehensive. She was still struggling to absorb last night's momentous news and its likely repercussions. Gabriel must be feeling even more at sea. She at least had suspected that mystery attached to her birth, while he'd had no such intimations about an uncle who for most of his life had played the puritan.

''ow would I know?' Martha was at her belligerent best.

'P'raps it's 'cause yer face 'as curdled the cream.'

Her quip drew no response since Elinor's nerves were stretched tight. She almost wished she had not pushed her search to its conclusion, for now she was caught in a web of her own weaving. When she'd embarked on this journey, she had thought to find an elderly gentleman of modest means who might welcome young companionship into his solitary life. But there was no elderly gentleman, no modest living. Instead there was a mansion of unimaginable proportions, a demesne so large it was only possible to cover it on horseback, and a master who had known nothing of either her or her mother. A master who was young, rich and heedless.

That was the nub of the problem. Gabriel was too young and too fascinating. Even at a distance she had found herself unwisely attracted, so how much worse would it be if she came to live close to him? Last night she had come perilously near to inviting his kisses. It was a salutary warning that told her very clearly she should not stay at Amersham. The most sensible course of action was to leave immediately. There was only one difficulty; she had no idea where to go or how she would survive. And meanwhile an impatient duke commanded her attendance.

Thirty minutes later she was ushered into the duke's study, the very same room in which he had surprised her holding the locket and precipitated this entire maelstrom. He was not alone and Elinor was disconcerted to see he was accompanied, not by Mr Jarvis which she might have expected, but by an unbending matron of some fifty years whom she had last seen on race day. The woman stared at her as she hovered in the doorway.

'Elinor, I bid you good morning.' Gabriel's use of her full name made clear he intended to recognize their unusual relationship.

His voice sounded just a little too hearty as he beckoned her into the room. 'Come, I would like you to meet my aunt, Lady Celia Frant.'

As if a servant at Amersham would not already know the woman, Elinor thought. But how determined the duke appeared that Nell the dairymaid should vanish as swiftly as she had arrived.

'I think you have already made the acquaintance of Roland, Lady Frant's son.'

Gabriel looked slowly from one guest to another and seemed perplexed how best to continue. He cleared his throat. He was nervous, Elinor thought. Gabriel nervous? What exactly was coming? It couldn't be pleasant judging by his aunt's hostile expression. He cleared his throat again and this time looked directly at her.

'Lady Frant has generously agreed to move from the Dower House to the Hall – for a time at least – so that you may have the necessary chaperon. I am shortly to travel to Brighton and from there will accompany the Regent when he returns to Carlton House. While I am absent, Lady Frant will guide you in the way you should go on.'

What was he saying? That while he disported himself in London, she must live at the Hall, idling her days away, her only company this dragon of a woman busily breathing fire with every stiff fibre of her body. He was mad to think she would agree to such a proposition. Taken aback by the sudden turn of events, she stammered out the first words that came into her head. 'And the dairy?'

He hardly seemed to register her bewilderment, but continued with what appeared to be a prepared speech. 'You will relinquish your post in the dairy as of now. A maid has already packed your belongings and moved them to a room which has been made ready for you. I thought the west tower? It has an excellent view of the lake and the woods beyond.'

Bewilderment turned to annoyance. His conduct was high-handed in the extreme. Without consulting her, he had decided on her future and acted upon it.

'But –' she began to say when Celia Frant interrupted her brusquely. 'You would do well, my dear, to banish from your mind the fact you have ever been a dairymaid.' There was a visible shudder. 'And well to forget the unhappy circumstances of your birth. You are fortunate indeed that His Grace has decided to recognise you and treat you accordingly.'

Elinor could have struck the woman. Instead she said in a voice she had to fight to keep steady, 'I am proud of my birth – at least on my mother's side. I would not be so discourteous as to venture comment on the parent who abandoned her.'

If Celia Frant could be said to reel, she did so on hearing this undisguised heresy. She cast a look of anguish in the duke's direction, but he ignored her and once more spoke directly to Elinor. 'Rehearsing old history is unhelpful in our present situation. It would seem you are partly a Claremont, Elinor, and as such you should be housed appropriately. I have decided it would be best for you to live at the Hall, at least until you have had time properly to consider your future.'

'It is certainly a more sensible idea than living at the Dower House.' Lady Frant had recovered sufficiently to interject this waspish comment.

So the duke had approached this disagreeable woman to house her in her own home, Elinor thought, and she had refused. But why would she prefer an illegitimate nobody to be living in ducal splendour? The answer to the question swiftly presented itself. The door of the study had been left open and the difficult conversation brought to a halt by the sound of sharply clicking boots.

Roland Frant appeared at the door and forgetting the polished manners of which he was so proud, spoke curtly. 'What is this I've been hearing from Jarvis? That Nell Milford is a Claremont?'

'Always a little late, Roland,' the duke said sweetly, 'but do come in.'

Since his cousin had already joined them, the comment was barbed. Roland, though, had been so thoroughly shaken by the news the butler had imparted that the duke's words had little effect.

'I don't understand how a dairymaid has become our cousin.'

'Not a legitimate cousin.' His mother's voice came as sharp as a newly honed knife.

'But still...'

'You do not need to understand, Roland,' the duke

muttered irritably, 'simply accept that such is the case. Nell Milford is no longer. Let me present Elinor Milford. She will be moving into the west tower as of today.'

But Roland would not be silenced, his face a study in shocked propriety. 'Surely you cannot intend to house a young, single woman here. She would be better by far at the Dower House where my mother can act as chaperon.'

'That won't be necessary.' Lady Frant was swift to intervene. 'I am to be Miss Milford's chaperon but here at the Hall.'

'So you see, Roland, you need be anxious no longer.' Gabriel's face wore its most saturnine expression.

'I am not happy with this arrangement, Mama.'

'It need not concern you,' his mother said repressively. 'I shall bear Miss Milford company for the next few weeks – until she has had time to plan her future in the light of her changed circumstances.'

It was evident to Elinor that she was not to live at the Dower House for one reason alone. Celia Frant did not want her son under the same roof as an imposter. She must fear his forming a *tendre* for a woman she considered wholly ineligible. Obviously she entertained no similar fears for Gabriel and she was right. The duke's taste in women ran to eye-catching beauties. Elinor knew herself to be passably good looking, but she was no diamond of the first water. Her mouth was too generous and she was far too tall. Why, she could reach the duke's chin if she were to come close to him. Which she would not do. Ever again.

As she stood there, a reluctant fourth player in a quarrelsome quartet, she felt indignation limp away and a great weariness take its place. She had spent most of the night in that miserable cellar, then at five had begun work in the dairy. She was still overwhelmed by the knowledge that had come to light and all she wanted was sleep. She presumed that as Miss Elinor Milford, relative of the Duke of Amersham, she would be allowed that luxury. She would sleep, she decided, and then consider what to do when her bemused brain could once more think rationally.

A maid was waiting outside the study to conduct her to the turret room, the same maid who had packed her belongings from the little attic, and the same who had shared the supper table with her in the servants' hall the previous evening. What a long time ago that seemed. It was hardly surprising the girl was glancing at her curiously. Elinor supposed the servants' quarters were abuzz with gossip, for nothing so outlandish could ever have happened at Amersham before.

⌒

Roland escorted his mother back to the Dower House to collect such belongings she deemed necessary for a prolonged stay at the Hall. His head was still reeling from what he'd learned that morning. He had suspected for a while that Elinor might originate from superior stock, perhaps from a family fallen on hard times – that wasn't uncommon in the countryside – but he could never have envisaged she had Claremont blood running in her veins. For a long while he walked in silence beside his parent.

At last he said, 'Mama, do you think it wise that Elinor lives at the Hall?'

'I don't think it wise she lives anywhere in the vicinity,

but the duke is adamant that she is at least partly family and we cannot turn her away.'

'But would it not be better that she stay with us at the Dower House?'

'I am a little tired of hearing this refrain, Roland. Why do you persist in it? Do you have an interest there?'

His mother's suspicions occasioned an angry flush. 'No, indeed, Mama. I have no wish to become leg-shackled for many years and when I do I will choose a bride of equal birth to my own.'

'I am glad to hear it. I wish your uncle had thought likewise before he brought disgrace upon us. The Claremonts should not be forced to suffer an illegitimate pauper in their midst.'

'Those are harsh words.'

'There can be no room for sympathy when the name of Claremont is threatened. You should know that.'

'I do, but Miss Milford is charming – though not our equal,' he added hastily, 'and I feel strongly that living at the Dower House would be more conducive to the young lady's welfare.'

'She is unlikely to stay long at the Hall and I doubt she will come to harm. I shall be there, do not forget. And while I am there, I shall use it to our very best advantage.'

'I don't understand.' His tone was plaintive.

Celia Frant looked into the distance and sighed heavily. 'You so rarely do, Roland. You have little understanding of where your best suit lies and it is as well I have an eye to it. While Nell, Elinor Milford, whatever she chooses to call herself, lives at the Hall, I will have the chance to carve out a niche for myself and for you. I shall make sure I am useful in every way possible and so acclimatise the household to the idea of a more permanent arrangement.'

Roland felt bemused, but did not wish to incur his mother's wrath by demanding an explanation. For some minutes they walked the long, winding drive in silence again and then unable to contain himself any longer, he burst out, 'What kind of arrangement?'

'Simply that Gabriel Claremont is unwed and likely to remain so. His excessive living is well-known and even if he does not return to the dangers of soldiering, he is almost certain to court an early death. He should never have inherited, a younger son of a younger son. He has no more right to the dukedom than you.'

'I am his heir, Mama.'

'And as his heir you should be far more involved in the running of the estate, and more familiar with the routine of the household. The servants should know that you are next in line and treat you as such.'

'And you think that going as chaperon to Miss Milford will forward this plan?'

'It will make a beginning. I am convinced the girl's stay will be short and I mean to continue at the Hall long after she has gone. I intend to carve out a foothold for us and make our advance that much easier.'

Roland looked thoughtful, unsure whether or not to voice the further concerns which had come to mind. In the end, he decided to be brave. 'Are you not afraid that Gabriel might fall in love with her and make her his wife?'

'Such sentimental nonsense! Dukes do not fall in love.

He might make her his mistress since he has no notion of what is due to his state. But he would know better than to marry her. He has her history to hand. Like mother, like daughter.'

'Again, Mama, that is very harsh.'

'I will confess I am angry, deeply angry, at what has transpired. I knew nothing of my brother's by-blow and never thought I would have to stoop to associating with her.'

'Did you have no idea of Uncle Charles' secret?'

'Of course I did not. Are you suggesting he would have told a sister, years his junior, such a shocking tale? If he told anyone, it would have been Hugo. As his only brother and near to him in age, that might have made some sense. It is possible he told Hugo's son when Jonathan came of age. But they are all dead and we cannot know.'

'Do you think Aunt Louisa knew her husband's history?'

'Louisa is an earl's daughter. If she suspected, she would have had the sense and the dignity to say nothing.'

They walked up the short pathway to the front entrance of the Dower House. Roland lifted the latch, but before pushing the door open he felt bold enough to ask, 'Do you think she should be told now?'

'That will be up to Gabriel. For myself I would advise him to say nothing. Charles is no more and Louisa has returned to Northumberland to the bosom of her family. Why stir waters that can remain calm – especially as this particular little storm is almost certain to blow itself out before it has properly begun.'

Chapter Thirteen

It took several days for Elinor to stop waking before five and scrambling into her clothes. Even after a week she could not accustom herself to Alice bringing her hot water each day and a morning cup of chocolate. Nor to the spacious room she now occupied with its stunning vista of water and wood. Every morning she opened her eyes to the murals splashed across the ceiling above and wondered where on earth she was. Alice had been her lifeline in relaying in minute detail what was being said among the servants about this extraordinary turn of events. No one seemed to bear her ill will, which was comforting, but several of the men had expressed a view on Elinor's preferment that Alice did not want to repeat. Suffice to say the duke's morals had come into question.

But the duke was the least of Elinor's problems. He seemed to be playing least in sight and though he had not yet left for Brighton, he was out on horseback for days on end, apparently checking the furthest reaches of his estate. On occasion he stayed overnight at whatever hostelry was nearest, and when next she saw him he would be striding mud-splattered from the stables to go directly to the bailiff's office or to his own study. He seemed to spend an inordinate amount of time on estate affairs for someone who had previously shown little interest. Elinor could only assume he was deliberately keeping out of her way and out of the way of his aunt. That at least was understandable for it was Celia Frant she found most wearing.

It was nothing the woman actually said, but in her company Elinor always felt a fraud. She guessed that Lady Frant was hoping her unwelcome guest would not be at Amersham for long and it was a hope she shared. The luxury of being served by an army of retainers was a guilty pleasure and living in splendour a delight. But she was bored. She was used to work, not shuffling her way through aimless hours interspersed by the occasional walk, the occasional book or journal, the odd hour's practice on the pianoforte. It was a dawdling life and she was desperate to feel useful once more.

One evening, after enduring yet another silent meal, she decided to meet the challenge head on and turned to Lady Frant as they were leaving the table.

'While I am here, your ladyship, I would like to be of some practical help at Amersham. I was wondering if there is anything I might do.'

Celia Frant sniffed. 'Hardly. The duke has a staff of over a hundred. There is even a new dairymaid hired in your place, I believe, so butter making is no longer an option.'

'I was not thinking of butter making.' Elinor flushed. 'But perhaps something in the house.'

'Dusting? I think not, there are housemaids a plenty for that.'

The wilful misinterpretation of her words only strengthened her resolution. 'I was thinking there might be opportunities for fine sewing. I am generally believed to be an accomplished needlewoman.'

'Like your mother, you mean.'

The tone was derisive, but she refused to be silenced. 'My mother was a talented painter, Lady Frant.'

'If you say so, my dear.'

'I have the proof. Did you ever see the miniatures she painted of herself and her lover?'

Elinor intended to shock and she had. Celia's face grew crimson. 'You would be well advised never to allude to such immorality again. Such a shocking past should stay buried.'

Elinor's head was high. 'I do not consider my past *is* shocking since I am certain I was conceived in love. No woman could paint with such tender feeling and not love the subject of her painting.'

Lady Frant stalked to the door. 'This conversation is improper in the extreme. Please never refer to such things again.' The door closed behind her with a sharp smack.

She knew she had gone too far. Celia Frant was deeply unhappy with her presence at Amersham and the disgraceful nature of her brother's affair only added to the flames. She should have trod lightly and shown greater sensitivity to the older woman's feelings. But she could not bring herself to like her and, though during the daylight hours they managed to avoid each other almost completely, the evenings were a trial for them both.

⌒

Halfway through the week a diversion occurred to lighten

her spirits. The carrier from Steyning arrived, his cart crammed full with boxes of every shape and size, but all fastened with fancy ribbons. It took three footmen to heave them up the steep steps to Elinor's tower room.

'Are these all for me?' she gasped, when one by one the men deposited their burdens.

The youngest footman grinned. He was still young enough to enjoy getting presents himself. As soon as he left, she tore eagerly at the first box. Within minutes she was admiring a dress of eau-de-nil sarsnet flounced with French trimmings. She held it up against herself and danced around the room, the frills of the gown swaying and rustling to her movements. Then on to the next box and the next and the next. It was not long before the bed and floor were littered with gowns for every occasion, along with matching pelisses, spencers, gloves, reticules made from the finest silk and even a velvet cape of forest green: everything indeed a young lady might need to make a splash in society.

In the middle of this glorious havoc, there was a soft tap at the door and Alice came in. The grapevine had been busy in the servants' quarters and, as soon as she heard the news, she had hurried to her mistress. In seconds she was as busy as Elinor, drawing from the remaining bandboxes shoes for walking and for dancing, for inclement weather and for good, along with poke bonnets sporting the brightest ribbons and charming confections of gauze masquerading as hats. One particular Norwich shawl sent her into ecstasies until Elinor rescued it from her frantic clasp. In the very last bandbox they uncovered a cache of silk stockings and three of the laciest nightgowns Elinor had ever seen. Their excited chatter ceased. They were kneeling on the floor facing each other and exchanged a look which bridged the gulf between mistress and maid. Such intimate items provoked the same thought in each young woman, but it was Elinor who voiced it.

'Who could have ordered such things?'

'Lady Frant?' Alice suggested hopefully.

'I would think it highly unlikely. But perhaps her lady's maid?' She was desperate for there to be a respectable explanation.

'More like it's Mrs Lucas. She's probably been told to supply a wardrobe for you, miss, now you're Quality.'

'Yes, Mrs Lucas,' Elinor agreed gratefully. If that were so, the housekeeper had admirable taste and an amazing eye for style and fit.

'How very thoughtful of her to have covered – well, just about everything.' She laughed uncertainly, but then the morning dresses, the walking dresses, the evening apparel regained her attention and soon she and Alice were carefully hanging these precious acquisitions in the hitherto empty wardrobe. When at last her maid left, Elinor stood gazing at her new riches, entranced by the softly shimmering silks and satins. Even the simple muslins were of the finest weave and all chosen to compliment the dark hair and pale skin of her Irish ancestry.

That evening she chose to wear the pale apricot figured silk with cream kid slippers and a fillet of tiny cream blossoms woven through her dark curls. As she entered the dining room, Celia Frant stared in surprise. She was accustomed to sitting down to dinner with a grey mouse and the girl who took her chair opposite looked complete to a shade, her hair dressed *à la mode*, courtesy of Alice's perusal of *La Belle Assemblée*. But rigid upbringing ensured that Lady Frant ignored the transformation.

Once more the duke made no appearance and by the evening's slow end Elinor felt miserably deflated. The moment she had donned the exquisite gown and Alice had dressed her hair so beautifully, she had felt like the giddy girl she had never been. She had tripped down the tower stairs with happiness in her soul, longing to laugh and dance, to be lively and bright, to feel the warmth of male approval. Instead she had sat in cold silence with a woman who deplored her. Back in her room she took the flowers from her hair and bundled the dress sadly away.

~

The next morning she could not be persuaded to step out in one of the smart walking dresses she and Alice had unpacked only yesterday. Instead she dressed herself in the familiar grey poplin and kept to her room. By two o' clock she was thoroughly weary of the tower, of the Hall, of herself. She wandered over to the window and stared blankly out at the vista: the stables to one side, the rose garden to the other, and right before her, acre upon acre of rolling green. The sound of a horse and carriage being driven hard came to her ears and in a minute a high-perch phaeton appeared around the corner of the house, travelling at a spanking pace. It pulled to a sharp halt at the rear entrance. The duke had arrived. She watched him jump from the carriage, looking down on the scene from her turret like a princess waiting for rescue. At that moment, he looked up and grinned. He had read the fairy tale, too. The grin decided her. She would beard him in his den. She gave him a while to settle and then made her way to his study.

'Come in.' The tone was unpromising, but his expression lightened when he looked up from his desk and saw her.

Elinor walked a few paces into the room. 'May I speak with you, Your Grace?'

'You're here, so by all means speak.'

He waved his hand towards one of the easy chairs, but she preferred to stay close to the door. She wasn't at all sure how he would respond to her proposal.

'How do you find your new life?' His question stopped her as she was about to begin the small speech she had prepared.

'That is why I have come.'

'You are well, though, I take it?' He had risen from the chair, but remained by his desk.

'Perfectly well, but if I am to stay longer at the Hall, I need employment.'

His eyebrows rose and she hoped he wouldn't be tempted to tell her the position of dairymaid was now filled. But he said nothing and she went on, 'I had thought of needlework, but it appears you have all the seamstresses and embroiderers you could possibly need. But the library – I think it a room that would benefit from attention.'

'You would know, of course,' he said lightly, 'having already plundered its depths.'

She flushed slightly, but continued to push her point. 'You would not mind if I began to catalogue the library contents?'

'You will first have to equip yourself with a handful of feather dusters.'

She relaxed. It looked as though the duke did not intend to over-rule her. 'Mrs Lucas has promised me as many as I need.'

'You'll need suitable clothes, too. I hope you don't mean to wear the gowns that arrived this week.'

'How?...' she began to ask. 'It was you that sent them?'

The customary saturnine expression flitted across his face. 'Who else?'

She felt unbearably flustered, thinking of the silk stockings and the lace nightgowns. 'I didn't know,' she stammered. 'I thought one of the female members of the household. They fitted so perfectly.'

His smile this time was genuine. 'Exactly!'

She blushed bright red and then remembered her manners. 'Thank you, Your Grace.'

'Should we not drop the title? Call me Gabriel – it is my name.'

'Thank you, Gabriel,' she repeated. 'It was most kind in you.'

He had enjoyed putting her out of countenance, but he had also gone out of his way to make her feel at home in a world which was new and strange to her. Instinctively, she moved forward meaning to clasp his hand in gratitude, at the same time as he began walking towards her. But when they were within a few feet of each other, they came to an abrupt halt. It was as if there was a force field between them that neither could cross. His eyes rested on her – unwavering, penetrating, as though he could not wrench his gaze away. For what seemed an age he stood without moving and simply looked. She felt her skin gather heat until her whole body was aflame. A pain deep within dissolved her stomach to water; her legs, too, gradually lost all strength. And still he continued to look and she to bear his scrutiny, caught in a spell neither could break.

She forced herself to speak, to take control of the situation. 'I should leave you in peace and go to find Mrs Lucas.'

Her voice seemed to jerk him from his dream. 'Ask her for anything you wish.' Then as an afterthought, 'And change that hideous dress!'

She managed a brief smile before she escaped from the room.

Chapter Fourteen

When she had gone, Gabriel remained very still. His strategy wasn't working. He had ridden more miles than he cared to remember this last week and stayed in hostelries that had no right to the name, all to ensure he saw as little as possible of Miss Milford. He had hoped that by staying away he would weaken the pull she exerted. But the first time he'd come face to face with her in – what was it, seven days, eight days? – he'd been unable to keep his eyes away. She had been dressed in that dowdy mouse costume of hers, but it hardly mattered. She was far too attractive and he was far too tempted.

She wasn't classically beautiful but her face entranced him, the cloud of dark hair framing the pale, pale skin and those misty green eyes, eyes that looked directly at him, deep into his soul as though they would plunder his every secret. He liked her too. He liked her spirit and determination, liked that she would not be beaten. But liking and lust were a dangerous combination and he had no idea how to deal with it. He could not spend another week in fruitless wandering and the prospect of travelling to Brighton was no longer tempting: the same people, the same houses, the same social round. It would be unbearably tedious, but his erstwhile companions were waiting for him and he supposed he must go. Just not yet. For the moment he would rather take his chance at Amersham, despite the risk of living so close. At least she had found herself an occupation which would keep her busy and at a distance. He must do the same.

ᶜᵔ

Some days later when he passed the library, she was at work. If he had known she intended such an early start, he would have chosen a different route that morning. But she was already seated on the floor, several piles of books and papers at her elbow. Her skirts were spread around her and her hair tied back in loops across her ears. She looked demurely business-like, but when she heard his step and looked up, her generous lips widened into a smile and her eyes danced with fun.

'Have you any idea, Gabriel, how many books you possess on pig keeping?'

Good manners prevented him from walking on and instead he hovered in the doorway. 'No, tell me.'

'So far it is twenty-three and I'm still counting. You do keep pigs at Amersham?'

'The home farm produces some excellent bacon so I imagine we do, but I'm not personally into pig husbandry.'

'One of your ancestors evidently was.'

'One of yours, too,' he reminded her.

It seemed a good idea to stress their family connection, but the mention of her changed station appeared to make her ill at ease. She smoothed her skirts and then fidgeted with a few strands of hair that had come loose.

To cover her discomfort, he said in a rousing tone, 'How long do you intend to immure yourself in this dark and dingy place?'

She sat back on her knees. 'It's not at all dingy and I like the shadows. They're restful.'

'I have to break it to you that they are not shadows but cobwebs. Look.' And he brushed one away which had been dangling menacingly close to her face. 'I have an army of servants yet I also have cobwebs. But at least no spider.'

She jumped to her feet. 'Urgh. Is it on my face?'

'No,' he laughed, 'though you do have a very large smudge just here.' And he rubbed at her cheek with one finger.

Her face was soft to his touch. He wanted to run his finger down her cheek into the small white hollow at the base of her neck. That would be the craziest thing yet. It was all very well to dally with high born ladies while their husbands drank and gambled the hours away since they knew the stakes. They were natural courtesans. This girl, though, was as innocent as the month of May.

She flopped down on the floor once more, secure in the knowledge that cobwebs and their accompanying spiders had been banished.

'I found these old maps, do look,' she invited him. 'I couldn't be sure, but they appear to be of the Caribbean.' She patted the cushion beside her. 'What do you think?'

He had little option but to take the place she'd indicated. 'Yes, they're maps of the Caribbean. And this is one of Jamaica.'

'Why would you have a map of Jamaica in your library?'

'The Claremonts had a plantation on the island.'

Her forehead wrinkled in surprise. 'And do they still?'

'No. It was sold after my parents died there.'

She looked crestfallen but reached out to give his arm a squeeze. 'I am so sorry, Gabriel. I knew they had died young but I had no idea it happened so far away.'

'How could you? But don't distress yourself, it was all a long time ago. I was no more than four years old when it happened.'

'Then you didn't travel with them?'

'Jonathan and I were left behind at Amersham. Jamaica was far too unhealthy a place for young children.'

'But your mother and father? Why did they make such a perilous voyage?'

'My father was supposed to go alone. There had been a good deal of unrest among the slaves and the over-seers demanded someone with authority come out from England to settle the disputes before they flared into out-right rebellion.'

'And your father volunteered?'

Her words produced a scornful expression and when he spoke his tone was scathing. 'I doubt there was much voluntary about it. My father had to make amends for his unwise marriage. I told you that he eloped, didn't I? So it fell to him rather than to his older brother to brave the oceans. The heir had to be preserved.'

'And your mother? Surely it was not a place for a lady?'

'It was not a place for either of them. They caught dengue fever and died within a sennight of each other. She refused to let her husband go there alone. But that's love for you.'

There was a sourness in his voice that made her unsure how best to respond. Eventually she said, 'It's a very sad story. You were only a small boy at the time, but I hope you have some memory of them still.'

He said nothing. They were memories he did not want to bring to life and steered quickly back to their earlier conversation. 'You should not bury yourself in this mausoleum all day.'

'I don't, I promise. I walk every morning and most afternoons. But what of you?'

'What of me?'

'You should not bury yourself either. You seem always to be with the bailiff these days.'

He pulled a wry face. 'I've been trying to get to grips with estate management, but Joffey isn't the best mentor.'

'The fact that you are trying says much.'

'Is it possible that I've earned a special commendation? If so, it must be the first time in my life.'

'You never earned one as a boy? Wasn't your tutor encouraging?'

'My tutor, our tutor, was thoroughly indifferent. But he could hardly be blamed – he had little say in our upbringing. Charles Claremont ruled all.'

'That sounds forbidding.' There was a pause before she asked shyly, 'Were you *never* happy at Amersham?'

'There were lighter moments. The estate made a splendid playground with plenty of hideouts like the one I showed you. When Jonty and I managed to escape the iron hand of Uncle Charles, we roamed at will.'

'You make him sound a very strict guardian.'

'He was a bitter and tyrannical man – a despot, in fact.'

The words were stark and she looked appalled. He tried to sugar the pill. 'There was very little to like about my uncle, but living with Aunt Louisa would make any man surly, particularly if he'd been forced – as now seems likely – to abandon the woman he loved.'

'Then he showed you little affection?'

'None whatsoever. And Aunt Louisa, if anything, was colder. We were nuisances to them, burdens they had been left with by my parents' death. And they made us feel that burden every minute of every day. To be fair, being an unwilling guardian to two spirited boys is a test of anyone's temper.'

'Spirited as in naughty?'

'We were certainly guilty of mischief, but only what every boy worth his salt gets up to. I remember that once we stole one of his guns and that sent him into a paroxysm. Luckily it wasn't loaded. But we did get to stage a military parade up and down the drive for at least an hour before he caught us.'

'And then you became real soldiers.' A dark shadow crossed his face. 'Tell me about life in the army,' she said hurriedly.

He began to drum his hands on the carpet. 'Strangely enough, it was wonderful. Terrifying for much of the time, but wholly exhilarating. I would not have missed the Peninsular campaign for the world. There were privations aplenty, but they only served to make me realise I was alive.'

She looked wistful. 'It's true that men will face danger and hardship, but in some ways they are more fortunate. A woman could never experience one half of what you've known.'

'Not always fortunate. There are some things a woman escapes and a man cannot – the bonds of inheritance, for instance. I was forced to leave the army, forced to sell out after Charles decided to break his neck.'

She stared at him. 'That sounds as though you think your uncle's action was deliberate.'

'It's not unlikely. He died two months after the Battle of Vitoria. That was where Jonathan fell.'

He was seared by the old recurring pain, but for some reason he wanted to keep talking. 'My brother was always his favourite – far more biddable, far less difficult than me. Charles never had children of his own and Jonathan became his project.'

'It's strange he had no children.'

'It's ironic. That hit me the other day. Aunt Louisa must have been barren and the one child he had, he refused to acknowledge.'

'But as a girl I wouldn't have been much use as an heir.'

'Neither was Jonty in the end. That was Charles' final disappointment in life, I guess.'

'Perhaps he lost more than an heir,' she suggested tentatively. 'The strict discipline he imposed could have masked genuine love for your brother.'

'Hardly. It was as though Jonty was a cadet and Uncle Charles his commander.'

'And you?'

'I was considered worthless.'

'But you became a soldier,' she protested, her voice shocked. 'Hardly worthless. And now you are the owner of an enormous estate with hundreds of people depending on you. If your uncle were here, he would be made to eat his words.'

Without thinking, he moved closer. 'You have a fearlessness about you, Elinor, that I admire greatly.'

An awkward silence fell between them and her voice was unusually bright when she spoke again. 'These old maps are fascinating.'

'Fascinating,' he murmured.

'You're not looking!'

'Indeed I am.' He was unable to resist. Her eyes this morning were of the palest green and her fine black brows a splendid frame. He saw her cheeks fire red and dropped his glance immediately. But he continued to sit beside her as she leafed through the sheaf of old engravings she had found alongside the maps.

'The land your family owned must have been extensive.' She was pointing to a detailed drawing of the plantation. 'Look at the size and number of the fields and see how many cabins have been built for the slaves.'

She picked up another of the engravings and waved it in the air. It was the image of a black woman dressed in a long flowered skirt and a matching bandana. 'She doesn't seem rebellious. She looks almost happy...I wonder...oh, but...' And she held up the next sheet of paper for them both to see. It was a sketch of an overseer, his hair matted, his face scowling against the sun, hands large and rough and holding a whip.

'His body is contorted with anger.' She shivered slightly though the library was already warm from the morning sun. 'I would not wish to be under the control of such a one.'

He remembered finding that engraving as a child and having nightmares for weeks afterwards. And he could see that it had affected Elinor in the same way. She had a sensitivity to the visual that must come from her mother. Her mother. And Uncle Charles. That was the strangest business. Who would have thought it of such an authoritarian, such a martinet! But he could not always have been so. Once he must have been young and in love and the result was sitting very close, her shoulders touching his, her hands almost touching his. Actually touching if he, too, took hold of the engraving. He did and there was a momentary shock as his skin met hers. She looked up, her eyes startled but unfathomable.

'Forgive my clumsiness,' he said hastily. 'The picture is already fragile and I came close to tearing it. It's as well you are the archivist and not me.'

He longed to touch her again and a rush of feeling threatened disaster. But before he could succumb, the door opened to admit Celia Frant.

'Ah Gabriel, you're here.'

'As you see, aunt.' It was possibly the only time in his life he had been pleased to see his relative.

'Summers tells me the tailor awaits you in your room. He has travelled from Brighton and is anxious to return this day. I am sure our little friend is more than capable of spring cleaning alone.'

Gabriel got to his feet. He had stayed far too long. Over the past few days he had been successful in keeping his distance from Elinor – an hour at dinner each evening, the occasional brief acknowledgement if they passed in the house. But today his carefully constructed defences had fallen. It wasn't just that her beauty mesmerised him. He felt at ease in her company, that was the damnable thing. There was something about the girl that made him want to talk, to confide, in a fashion that was wholly foreign to him. That business about his childhood, for instance. He had told her his parents' deaths meant nothing to him, but she seemed to know differently. She had awakened memories he'd banished long ago.

Two small boys left to find their way alone in life. He remembered nights weeping into his pillow when only Jonty's arms around him could lull him to sleep. He remembered dreaming of his parents so vividly that he was sure they were there in the room with him. His mother, small and dainty, her delicate face framed by soft ringlets, smiling down with loving eyes. There she was at the door, kissing him as if she would never stop, and his father hoisting him up on his shoulders for a final farewell.

But the dreams always turned to nightmares. Time after time he was taken to a very different room. Large trees loomed at the window, their fronds waving wildly from the ocean gusts. It was hot, sticky, and the smell of disease pervaded everything. His mother and father were in the room, lying on separate beds; so many miles from home, so many miles from their children. Their skin was blanched, whiter than the sheets that covered them, white and glistening with sweat. They were ill, dying, and no one could save them.

Jonty had looked out for his small brother from the moment he realised their parents were not coming back. He had defended him from hostility, protected him from their guardians' anger. He was strong and courageous and even Charles had felt pride in the heir he had groomed. But Gabriel had been considered a shadow of his brother, one to be ruled by his uncle's iron fist and treated with disdain by his aunt. He had grown the necessary shell that over time had transmuted into physical courage – one could not else be a soldier – but the sorrows of childhood were not so easily forgotten. When Jonathan died, the only good thing, the only true feeling from a miserable past, died with him. No wonder he had felt forsaken.

For months he'd refused to think about his brother's death, refused to accept his loss, for then he could pretend that somewhere in the world Jonathan still lived. Instead he had thrown himself into every kind of rout and rumpus. That earlier madness might be over, but he never wanted to feel again and Elinor was a threat. Not that he would ever love her since he had not the capacity to love, but that she might become too important to him. He could not allow that to happen.

Chapter Fifteen

The next morning Elinor was alone at the breakfast table when a sharp rap on the window caused her to choke on a half-eaten muffin. To her amazement she saw Gabriel framed in the glass, beckoning her out of the house. He looked harassed and irritated in equal measure.

She hesitated. Yesterday in the library she had behaved imprudently and found herself in a difficult situation. He had a body to melt into if one were foolish enough, and it had been hard to remember that she was not, and that the bluest of blue eyes must not persuade her otherwise. This morning, though, she could hardly refuse his command and stopped only to fling a wool cape around her shoulders before making her way through the huge oak door that guarded the rear entrance of the Hall. The weather had turned cool and the July sky hung low and grey. She had hardly put her foot on the path when Gabriel grabbed her by the arm and towed her towards the sheltered enclosure of the walled garden. Several men were busily trimming the fan of peach trees which clung in delicate patterns to the walls of warm red brick. Planted squarely across the path ahead, Mr Hepburn, hands on hips, stood implacable.

'Elinor, do you know anything about this?' the duke demanded.

"This" turned out to be a wide scattering of earth and two large, ragged holes which between them had managed to upend a cluster of infant camellia bushes. She could have laughed aloud but for the head gardener's thunderous expression.

'I don't generally engage in digging,' she said calmly, 'and when I do, I find a spade is very helpful.'

'It's not you personally, miss,' the gardener puffed, shifting his bulk from one leg to another. 'It's the dawg.'

She looked bemused. 'The dog,' Gabriel interpreted. 'That benighted scrap of fur and bones belonging to my aunt.'

'Caesar? What about him?'

'Apparently you've been seen taking him for walks.'

'Twice, I've walked him twice. And –'

'Hepburn was wondering,' the duke said carefully, 'whether on the two walks you took with this animal, you noticed Caesar attacking these bushes.'

'Naturally it's just the kind of thing one does notice.' Her sarcasm was heavy. She was annoyed that she had been pointlessly called from her breakfast. 'I stood by and watched with interest while the dog effectively killed them.'

'I think we can take that as a no, Hepburn. I will speak to my aunt.'

'You better, Your Grace. If 'tis that narsty little termagant, I won't be responsible for what I do to 'im.'

Gabriel nodded brusquely and chivvied Elinor back

through the brick archway. Once outside the walled garden, he turned to her with an apologetic expression. 'I'm sorry to drag you from the house, but Hepburn was so incensed I feared he might suffer an apoplexy. I thought it best to defuse the situation.'

'I defused it?'

'Your mockery at least put an end to his complaints.'

Elinor's lips twitched into a wry smile. 'His guess is probably right. Caesar has a penchant for digging.'

'Why my aunt has to bring her wretched animal up to the Hall!'

'I believe Roland is at Hurstwood for some days and she cannot leave the dog on its own.'

'To my knowledge the Dower House has a battalion of servants.'

'Yes, but Caesar bites their ankles and they refuse to be left with him.'

'That dog has no discernment. What's wrong with Roland's ankles?'

'Why do you dislike your cousin so much?' She hadn't meant to say it, but it was a question she had long wanted to ask.

The duke's answer was candid. 'He is sly and manipulative. A born sycophant.' Her face must have expressed surprise at the forcefulness of his response since he finished by saying in a milder voice, 'Let's just say we don't deal well together.'

She thought it best not to pursue the topic and turned instead to the garden. 'Mr Hepburn grows the most amazing hibiscus.' They were passing the deep flower beds which lay beneath the breakfast room window.

'Just look at that beauty,' and she cupped one of the blooms in her hand and bent her head to study it. 'My mother would have loved to have seen these. She enjoyed growing unusual plants. Bath suffers from a deal of rain, but the climate is mild and she was successful with all kinds of tropical flowers.'

'You must miss her very much.'

'I loved her dearly,' she said simply.

His glance was gentle. 'You have had a painful time of it, Elinor. You lost a much loved parent, but you also lost an entire way of life. It was brave of you to leave Bath and make a new start.'

'You called me brave yesterday, too. Fearless, I think you said. I'm flattered that you think me so, but really I am not. Whereas you, you were a soldier – that takes true courage.'

He moved a little closer and his deep blue eyes were searching. 'There are different kinds of courage. To leave shelter and walk into the unknown is to my mind very brave.'

'Not when the only shelter offered is the poorhouse.'

He gave a low whistle. 'Was it as bad as that? Surely one of your acquaintance, one of your mother's acquaintance, could have helped you in your trouble.'

'There was nobody to whom I would confess my poverty.'

'After all those years in Bath you had no close friends?'

'None.' She looked up at him and studied his face, thinking how comfortable it would be if he were her friend. 'After she died, several of my mother's former customers very kindly invited me to stay with them, but I always refused.'

'Why was that?'

'I never felt it right. I had no way of returning their invitation and I would not have enjoyed playing the poor orphan.'

He smiled appreciatively. 'I'm sure you would not. But anyone less like a poor orphan is difficult to imagine.'

He was looking at her in a way that made her ache with hardly understood emotions. 'Here, have this,' and in an instant he had swooped down to pick the exquisite flower she had admired. She took the flower and felt his hands enfold hers. For a moment she was pressed to his body and his mouth was brushing the top of her head, his lips caressing the tangle of her hair. She was filled with the most intense longing, to fit her arms around him, to pull him closer and closer until she and he were one single body. She looked up and saw in his eyes the same naked desire.

'Your breakfast will be growing cold,' he said abruptly and ushered her into the house.

⌒

When she regained the breakfast room it was to see Lady Frant seated at the table, her face an ominous mask. Elinor was uncomfortably conscious of the flower she held.

'May I give you a little advice, my dear.' Her honeyed tone was at odds with her face. 'As a young and unattached woman, you cannot be too careful. Appearances are everything and it is wise to observe them. The duke has installed me as chaperon to lend you propriety, but dukes can be forgetful. They have a habit, too, of getting their own way and that is not always good for them or for others. Who better than you to know? We must work together, my dear, to ensure we keep Gabriel on the straight and narrow.'

'I am sure His Grace does not need advice from me.'

Any more, she reflected, than she needed advice from Celia Frant. She knew only too well the duke was capable of charming her into his arms and just as capable of walking away once he became bored. Ruin lay that way and she was not intending to travel the road her poor mother had trod.

'You could exert a beneficial influence, Elinor,' the woman said repressively, 'while you remain at Amersham.'

'My time here is likely to be short.'

'How is that?' Celia permitted herself a hopeful smirk.

'*The Morning Post* has several advertisements for a governess and I intend making my application today. I am without formal qualifications, but with the duke's name behind me I am confident I shall soon find a position.'

'You mean to go as a governess?' Disdain fought with surprise.

'Do you have a better plan, Lady Frant?' she countered and sailed to the door, looking a great deal more composed than she felt.

⌒

Once in her room, she was unable to settle. She could still feel Gabriel's body and she wished she didn't like the feeling quite so much. From the outset she had been defenceless against his physical charm and the pull was getting stronger by the day. But now she faced a more intractable problem; he was starting to creep into her heart and that would be impossible to defend. Whenever they talked, she felt herself being drawn closer, felt herself understanding more and more clearly the demons that tormented him. He had hardly spoken of his brother's death, but she sensed the depth of his loss and the desolation he had felt in stepping into Jonathan's shoes.

Of late he had appeared less troubled, exercising his authority more easily and seeming to take pleasure in running his vast estate. But what if he carried out his promise to travel to Brighton and found himself back in the bosom of the Regent's coterie? She wished he would not go. She wished he would. The contrary impulses played havoc with her mind. She wanted him to stay close, but it was a treacherous wish. He was a danger, and the better she knew him the more dangerous he became. It was imperative she leave Amersham as soon as possible since disgrace loomed if she stayed. She had been dissembling when she'd told Celia Frant that she intended to apply for a post as governess, but she must make good the pretence – and do so this very moment. She snatched up her pen and for the next half hour busied herself with the task.

⌒

Gabriel looked gloomily through the windows of the bailiff's office. There was nothing for it, he would have to leave for Brighton and soon. He appeared to have lost all self-control. He could not stay away from Elinor and when he was with her he could not resist the compulsion to hold her as close as he possibly could. He had never felt such overwhelming desire for any woman. He had called her a witch that night in the cellar and he'd been right. The spell she exerted on him was getting stronger all the time and now he was well and truly caught in her web. She had not spun it deliberately, had not set out to entrap him, but her very lack of guile increased her fascination.

And she was equally tempted, he was certain. It was an impossible situation that could lead only to disaster and a dreadful repetition of her mother's fate. He must leave Amersham and stay away until his infatuation had dulled. It was inconvenient certainly since he had been working hard on estate business and looking forward to seeing his efforts rewarded, looking forward to proving that she was right to have faith in him. There he went again, bringing everything back to Elinor. He needed a mind shift and his comrades in Brighton would provide it. But the thought of them – Hayward, Weatherby, Letitia Vine – made his soul shudder. He had not seen or heard of them this last month and not missed them for a minute. On the contrary, his days had been filled with a new and satisfying purpose, but his nights...his nights had been filled with a longing he could not assuage.

He must go, there was no other way. The devil was that he must delay his departure for a few days. He had an appointment with one of Joffey's henchmen, a Mr Henderson, the day after tomorrow. The wooden bridge over the lake, it seemed, was about to fall into the water and the bailiff had been urgent in persuading his master to substitute an iron construction. The bridge had stood for at least two hundred years and Gabriel suspected that rebuilding it was simply another way for Joffey to relieve him of his money. But he couldn't take the chance. He would leave for Brighton the day after seeing Henderson. Surely he could manage to keep out of her way for that short time.

Chapter Sixteen

Elinor rose early the next morning and made her way to the library. Until she received a response to her application she must busy herself in whatever way she could, though of late cataloguing the room's contents had lost its sparkle. She spread out her notebooks, sharpened her pens and hitched up her skirts. A small ladder stood ready for use. She climbed its steps meaning to begin at the top shelf of a new section, always the most difficult, but as she grasped the first of the heavy volumes she glanced through the window to the landscape beyond. A breeze had sprung up and sent the trees dancing and restless. She could almost hear the sigh of their leaves and she wanted to be there, walking beneath them, as far away from the house as possible, as far away from the duke as possible.

In less than half an hour she had changed into more respectable attire and was making for the western boundary of the Claremont estate. It was the most easily reached and beyond its fences she had spied an enticing tree-shaded path, which she was sure would lead to a river since she had seen glimpses of glittering water in the distance.

Amersham possessed a lake and fountains, but a river was alive. It would blow away the megrims and keep her mind from constantly wandering into dangerous territory. The weather continued overcast but once out of the house and on the path leading away from the west wing, her spirits improved. Thirty minutes' walk found her passing through the furthest field gate and leaving Claremont land.

The shaded path was perhaps a little too shaded on such a cloudy day, but the woods on either side were delightful. Bluebells had bloomed and faded, though red campion had taken their place and their perfume filled the air. The path was much longer than she had supposed, but distances were deceiving and she was sure she would come upon the river before too long. It took another hour of walking before she did and by then she was concerned to see the grey of the clouds turn to a stormy slate and to feel the first few drops of rain on her face. It won't be much, she told herself. July had been exceptionally dry and this day would be no different.

She walked along the river bank, watching the water's swirling circles chase each other downstream. A few more raindrops fell, a little heavier this time. She had drawn opposite a bundle of reeds that had been twisted and plaited in brilliant fashion. It was a nest and as she watched a kingfisher came in to land and stalked his way around the surrounding muddy platform. He had seen her from the sky and had not liked her intrusion. She would turn here, she decided, and leave him in peace. But just as she began to retrace her steps, an enormous crack of thunder directly overhead alarmed both her and the bird. The kingfisher rose in the air, its bright blue feathers shining against the dark sky. A jagged flash of lightning followed. Her pulse quickened. She was a long way from home and she would find little shelter by the river.

She hurried back along the bank, intent on finding a place that might provide at least a partial shield from the rain. The storm was worryingly loud and increasing in volume all the time, the lightning constant now, illuminating the darkness like the stage of a theatre. She had almost reached the point where river and woodland paths met when a great fork of light pierced the sky and hurtled to earth, crashing into the trees ahead and stripping leaves and bark from a tall elm just yards in front of her. A large branch cracked loudly and fell to the ground, effectively blocking her path back through the woods. She stood paralysed; it had missed her by inches. She tried to gather her wits but was so thoroughly shocked that she found herself motionless in the torrential rain. In the distance she thought she heard a noise – was that the sound of galloping hooves? Then a voice calling to her.

Gabriel cleared the fallen branch with feet to spare and pulled his horse to a sharp halt. He slid to the ground as thunder cracked and crashed over their heads. The mare's eyes were rolling wildly and before he could seize the reins, she had bolted into the distance. He cursed and grabbed at Elinor's arm, pulling her roughly through the deluge and along the river bank in the opposite direction from where she had walked. He was moving so fast that she found it difficult to breathe and impossible to protect her beautiful skirts from the quagmire. She was about to tell him what she thought of this treatment when she saw what he intended. From out of the deep gloom a clearing emerged and in the clearing a small hut, dilapidated but once a place of shelter for woodsmen. It would provide refuge for as long as the storm continued. The terrified mare, she saw, had already found safety beneath its rough overhang.

The duke had not spoken a word as they'd fought their way along the river path, but once he had banged the door of the hut behind them, he burst out, 'What possessed you to walk this distance and on such a day?'

'I could hardly know I would encounter the worst storm for months,' she retorted, bewildered by his tone.

'A glance at the sky should have been sufficient. And why wander so far from the Hall?'

'It was an adventure.'

'I can see that,' he said caustically. 'An adventure that might have cost you your life.'

'I think you exaggerate.'

'Do I? That branch barely missed you. And God knows what else will come down before the storm is through. You are fortunate I've spent the morning visiting the most distant of my farms and it was on a whim I decided to return this way.'

Had he been escaping, too, she wondered, escaping from her? If so, he'd had his plans overturned and that might explain his anger. 'I suppose I should have known what to expect,' he was muttering. 'The river lies on my neighbour's land and you were trespassing – again!'

An impulse she hardly understood prompted her to confrontation. 'You seem unduly concerned with my trespassing.'

His mouth hardened into an uncompromising line. 'If I am, it is because your flouting of the proprieties shows an utter lack of consideration for others.'

The squabble had sprung out of nowhere, but Elinor did not hold back. 'I had forgot, Your Grace, that you inhabit such a high moral ground yourself that you are fully entitled to judge others.'

She turned away, looking through the dirt-encrusted window at the tempest beyond. They were quarrelling badly and she knew it owed it little to this morning's transgression. One endless minute followed another until the duke broke the impasse.

'Do you always walk alone?'

'Yes,' she answered curtly.

'And why is that? Would it not be better to take a companion? Alice, for instance?'

'I find my own company preferable.'

'Am I then to apologise for mine?'

For the first time in their encounter she felt a little ashamed. She was after all safe from the storm. 'Indeed, no. I am indebted to you for my rescue,' she managed.

'That must have been a difficult confession to make.' He smiled and the tension that had been so acute dissolved a little.

She felt his dark blue eyes on her – they were almost navy in their intensity – but she was determined to keep aloof. She could not afford to feel attraction. What she should feel was gratitude, she told herself, gratitude for rescuing her from this foolish walk, for providing a home, for helping her uncover the secrets of her birth.

'A penny for them?'

'I was thinking how grateful I am to you.'

When he looked astonished, she continued, 'It was generous of you to believe in me, to believe in my connection to Amersham. And most generous of you to make me welcome in your home.'

'What else would I do?'

'I can think of much. I might even now be walking back to Bath.'

'In your grey mouse dress?'

'It had much to commend it.'

'What precisely?'

'It was hard wearing,' she said defensively, 'and appropriate.'

His gaze travelled slowly over her figure. 'I find what you are wearing today far more appropriate.' She looked down at the gown of orange blossom silk and became aware for the first time how closely the rain had moulded it to her form.

The conversation stuttered to a close and they waited once more in uncomfortable silence for the rain to abate. The tumbledown building was chilly and she was wet to the skin. She tried but failed to repress the shivers that were growing greater by the minute. He looked across at her and stripped off his riding jacket.

'Allow me,' and before she could stop him, he had draped the coat around her shoulders.

She heard the steady beat of his heart close to hers. Without thinking, it seemed, he moved his hands upwards from her shoulders and softly cradled her head, smoothing back the damp cloud of hair framing the pale oval of her face.

'I am sorry if I was discourteous.'

'It's of no matter,' she protested, willing him to let her go, willing him to hold her.

'I am an awkward man when it comes to modest maidens. Let us be friends again,' and he gently brushed her cheek with his lips, feathering the edge of her mouth as he did so. She felt the familiar slow dissolve somewhere deep in her body.

'Of course I haven't met many maidens,' he attempted to joke, 'they tend to be fairly thin on the ground in the Regent's company.'

'Then you should visit Bath. They are plentiful there,' she joked back in an effort to cover her confusion.

He glanced down at her, his expression almost tender. 'I should like to visit if only to discover more of your history. Did your mother tell you nothing?'

'Virtually nothing. I could only ever be sure of one thing and that was her name, Grainne Milford. Now that it appears she never married, I can use the name and know it is rightfully mine.'

'It matters that much to you?'

'It would matter to you, if you had never been sure from where you sprung.'

'You're right...Grainne,' he mused, 'it's a lovely name and has to be Irish. Do you know anything of your Irish relatives?'

The conversation had become unexceptional and her pulse mercifully slackened. 'Hardly anything. One of our customers made it her business to consult the Peerage and told me once that my mother must be the youngest daughter of an Irish peer, but she could have been mistaken.'

'No,' he said slowly. 'I don't think so.' He was thinking hard. 'Milford? I recall there was an Irishman of that name – in the Royal Horse Artillery, I believe. The Irish breed the finest horses. He hailed from Lismore. That could well be your mother's ancestral seat.'

'Perhaps, but I have no intention of crossing the Irish Sea to find out.'

'Don't tell me the spirited Miss Milford can be defeated by a stretch of water,' he teased.

'I would travel there if I wanted, but I don't.'

'Because?'

'Because my mother fled Ireland to escape her family. I don't know her reasons, but I suspect her father wished to sell her to the highest bidder. She was very beautiful. She was adamant that she would never return to Ireland and I have no wish to visit the family or their estate – they mean nothing to me.'

'Yet Amersham does?'

'Yes, it does. A great deal. It's where I've discovered who I really am. If I had no other reason to love it, that would be sufficient.'

'Then you will not be thinking of leaving us just yet?'

She took time to adjust the drying folds of her gown before she answered. 'I *must* leave. Our agreement was that I stayed until I'd had time to consider my future.'

'And have you considered?'

'I have applied for a post in Malmesbury.'

Standing with his back to the door, his powerful body seemed to block her departure. 'What kind of post?' he asked belligerently.

'I hope to go as governess.'

'As governess – as drudge, do you not mean? A drudge at twenty pounds per annum.'

'Twenty five pounds,' she corrected. 'It is a most superior household.' Her wide mouth broke into a smile, but he did not respond. Instead he grabbed her hands and clasped them hard. 'You do not have to work, Elinor,' he said fiercely. 'Amersham will keep you in comfort.'

'That is most generous, but I *must* work. It would not suit me to be without employment. Surely you can understand, you were yourself a soldier.'

'But no longer.' He let her hands drop and walked towards the window, staring out at the trees misshaped and contorted by the wind. 'Stay here,' he said urgently. 'Stay at Amersham and help me run the estate.'

'I cannot do that!' she said dazedly.

Gabriel was looking as dazed as she. His words seemed to have shocked him as much as Elinor and he had evidently not known they were coming. He began to pace up and down the small hut and after a dozen turns, walked back to the window and peered through its grimy glass.

'The rain appears to have eased at last,' he said tightly. 'I think we should attempt our return.'

Once outside, he called the mare from her shelter and offered Elinor his hand to mount. She knew she should refuse to go with him, but her legs were so weary she felt unable to walk another step. She allowed herself to be thrown into the saddle and in a second Gabriel had leapt up behind her and was nudging the horse forward, away from the blocked lane and towards open fields. His arms at first cradled her in a loose embrace, but gradually the mare's gentle rocking melded their figures closer and closer together. At each new field he was forced to bend in order to unlatch the gate, his hard form leaning into hers. She felt flushed, disturbed, her emotions hopelessly out of control – this was the very reason she should have refused the ride. It was as though she travelled in a dream, unaware of her surroundings and fixed only on the touch of his body. Unconscious of the miles passing, she was astonished to find they had arrived back on Amersham land and were journeying up the Hall's long, winding drive.

He helped her dismount, but did not look at her. Turning away to gather up the reins, he said over his shoulder, 'You have only a short walk from here. My advice would be a hot bath and warm clothes.' And without another word he strode towards the stables.

⌒

'Was that Gabriel I saw you with?'

Taken aback, she turned to face Roland. She tried to look welcoming, but his first words made it difficult. 'I think you must know it was,' she said sharply.

He looked ruffled by her tone. 'I have no wish to upset you, Elinor,' he protested. 'My only desire is to protect.'

She was not disarmed. She did not wish for protection, least of all from Roland Frant. There was no stopping him though. 'I am sure my cousin can be the most charming of companions,' he was saying, 'but he can also be the most dangerous – at least for a girl such as yourself.'

The hairs on her neck bristled to attention. 'What exactly do you mean – a girl such as myself?'

He had the grace to look uncomfortable. 'Well, my dear, your story is a little irregular, would you not say? In cases such as yours, it is wise to be particularly careful of even the smallest breath of scandal.'

Her face registered growing anger, but he ignored the storm signs. 'I am not saying you would encourage such a thing but Gabriel is arrogant and unthinking. He is used to women yielding to him and thinks of nothing but his own pleasure. He could easily ruin your prospects without a second thought.'

'My prospects, as you term them, are my own affair, Roland. But since you are so concerned, let me reassure you that I feel nothing more for the duke than grateful friendship. And however he may act with other women, I am sure I need have no fear for myself.'

He bridled. 'Let us hope you are right. I had no intention of causing distress, but I would be lacking in my duty if I did not warn you.'

'You have done so and now let it lie. If you will excuse me, I must return to the house.'

She left him looking slightly absurd in the middle of the carriageway and thought she had probably made an enemy, but he had infuriated her with his insinuations and she had been unable to hide her feelings. What upset her most, though, was that he had spoken a truth she did not wish to acknowledge.

Chapter Seventeen

'You must devise a plan as quickly as possible, Mama.'

Roland plunged into the drawing room of the Dower House out of breath and slightly unkempt. He had almost run down the drive in the hope of finding his mother still at home. She was packing a small basket to take back with her to the Hall.

'Gabriel is becoming just a little too enamoured with our unwelcome guest. I caught them just now riding together – on one horse!'

'I trust you put a stop to such flagrant conduct.'

'Naturally. He dismounted when he saw me. He must know I had no intention of leaving him alone with her, but I will not always be around.'

'I understand that, Roland, but you must not think me unaware. I have watched this unfortunate intimacy grow and made my plans accordingly. Miss Milford has spoken of her intention to find work, but that will not be a permanent solution to our problem. If her employment is unsuccessful, she could come back at any time and Gabriel is quite capable of seeking her out wherever she goes. It is a husband we need. A husband will take her off our hands for good.'

'That may be difficult.'

'Do not be such a faint heart,' his mother scolded. 'I already have such a one in mind. A Mr Ferrers. He is a respectable man, a lawyer I believe, but nevertheless enjoying considerable success as his practice expands. I know for a fact that he is looking for a wife and when he meets Elinor, I am sure he will take a liking to her. She is a little gawky – I find men generally balk at tall women – but attractive enough in a foreign kind of way. The courtship need only be brief. With a little encouragement, he will admire her sufficiently to make an offer, I am sure.'

'And Elinor?'

'She should be delighted with such a respectable marriage. A girl in her position cannot be too choosy and Mr Ferrers will provide a comfortable home. He is coming to tea at the Hall tomorrow and she will need to look her best. I will tell her the good news before dinner this evening.'

~

'What? Let me get this clear, Lady Frant. You have invited a man to tea so that he can view me?'

Celia Frant shuddered. 'You are unnecessarily coarse, and I would certainly not phrase it so. It is simply an opportunity for him to meet you. You would do well to make yourself available and amenable.' This last was said in a severe tone. Elinor's expression promised anything but amenable.

Lady Frant sailed smoothly along as though she were not at this moment encountering unbridled hostility. 'You never know, my dear, you may find you go on very well together. And in a short time it could lead to a respectable offer. Mr Ferrers is a professional man, it's true, but he is doing exceptionally well in his business and has already acquired a sizeable house and a stable of thoroughbreds.'

'And I am to join them? Tomorrow's little tea party is by way of being a reconnaissance mission for Mister, whatever his name is.'

'Mr Ferrers,' Celia said in a quelling tone. 'It would be wise to remember his name.'

'A reconnaissance mission,' Elinor repeated, 'so he can pick over the goods before deciding on a definite purchase.'

'Really, your language does you no credit. You would do well to be pleasant to him.'

'And you would do well to cease meddling in my affairs.'

'How dare you accuse me of meddling! I would never have invited Mr Ferrers if I had not known the duke's concern over your future.'

'The duke asked you to invite this man?'

'Not exactly. But marriage is the most sensible solution to the predicament we find ourselves in. I have simply helped matters along.'

'The duke has made known his concerns for my future!' Elinor exclaimed wrathfully. 'We will see about that.'

She banged out of the drawing room and rushed down the stairs and out through the huge oak front door. She went first to the estate office, which was locked and empty, then on to the stables. The grooms were mystified by her appearance since the duke had left hours ago. Was she to walk over the entire estate in order to vent her spleen? Then she remembered the study. It was unusual for Gabriel to take refuge there until after dinner, but knowing of the invitation to Mr Ferrers he must have gone to ground already.

She burst through the door as the duke was pouring himself a very large brandy. He was hoping to sink into the liquor's warm embrace and blot from his mind yet another unsettling encounter with Elinor. He had kept himself on a tight rein in that cheerless shack, but only just. And then the ride home, his arms around her trim waist, her body leaning into his – it was too much to bear. As a servant she had lived her life at a distance unless, he thought drily, she was poking around in rooms in which she had no business. But then he'd brought her into those rooms to live right under his nose and the more he saw her, the more he wanted her; the more he wanted her, the less he could have her.

His thoughts lost themselves in a haze of remembered pleasure. She had no idea how lovely she was. Today he had longed to run his hands through that glorious mass of dark curls, longed to see those misty green eyes cloud with desire and to snatch more than will o' the wisp caresses from those lips. He had wanted her all to himself. He was about to get his wish.

'You are unbelievable!'

Surfacing slowly from his dreamlike state, his eyes flickered in surprise at the rigid figure that confronted him. 'Elinor? What has happened? You are upset.'

'Upset? No, I am not upset. But incandescent with rage

– certainly!'

'Sit down please,' he gestured towards the chair directly opposite, 'and tell me the problem.'

'I will not sit down and you yourself are the problem.' Her figure was stiff with fury and her eyes flashed fire.

'Then if you will not sit, I must stand. Exactly how am I a problem?'

'You have all the arrogance of your class,' she almost spat out.

'I think we must have established that already.' His languid tone concealed a rising irritation.

'You are haughty, controlling and utterly insensitive.'

'We could exchange insults all evening. Why don't you get to the point?' He was bristling now.

'I will, you can be sure. It is not enough that your family has marauded through the neighbourhood causing pain and sadness, but now years later you must bury the evidence.'

He seemed bemused. 'Bury the evidence?'

'Evidence of their wrongdoing. You and your relatives are determined to rid Amersham of my presence.'

He looked at her measuringly. 'First of all, my *family* did not go marauding. It was one individual – I presume you are referring to Charles – who now lies dead, and incidentally, unmourned. And secondly, if you are the evidence of his marauding, it seems to me that far from getting rid of you I have done all I can to make you feel welcome.'

For a moment Elinor looked shamefaced but only for a moment before she was on the attack again. 'Any welcome I've received has been conditional. It is clear to me that your family has always been determined to see me go from Amersham. I have already begun my own arrangements to leave – I told you as much a few hours ago. But that isn't good enough. No, you have to control me to your own satisfaction. I must be married according to your dictate.'

'Married?' His tone lost its impassivity, but Elinor hardly noticed.

'The best of it is that before I reach this blessed state, I must be touted around the countryside to all the likely men who might be interested in taking an inconvenient base-born daughter off your hands.'

'What nonsense is this?'

He strode towards her as though he were about to shake her hard, but she stepped to one side and continued to speak in a voice tight with anger. 'I have it on the best of authority, your aunt's no less, the sister of my late and unlamented father. And lest I should think she is acting as a sole agent, she assures me it is your concern for my future that has prompted her to seek a mate for me.'

He looked confounded and said slowly, 'Are you telling me Celia has been matchmaking?'

'Matchmaking is far too romantic a term for the enterprise,' she said bitterly. 'And I cannot imagine this is fresh news to you.'

'You had better start imagining then. I have never, ever discussed the topic of your marriage with Celia let alone asked her to scan the neighbourhood for a likely husband.'

'If that is so, how does it come about that she has invited a Mr Ferrers to look me over tomorrow? He owns a stable of thoroughbreds, she tells me. I must make sure my teeth are shining and bright or he may pass me over.'

'This is ridiculous. Ferrers? Who the hell is he?' His annoyance was once more getting the better of him and he made no attempt to apologise for the oath.

'Who indeed? But I must not quibble. Your aunt seems well satisfied with her choice. An illegitimate child cannot expect to aim too high, you see, even when the prospective bridegroom is paid handsomely to take her off Claremont hands.'

He reached out and grasped her by the shoulders. 'You must stop this insane rant. I am not paying anyone to take you off my – our hands. Nor do I wish to impose a bridegroom on you.'

'Really? Your aunt is merely expressing the family sentiment, I'm sure. Tell her please that she is welcome to entertain Mr Ferrers to tea tomorrow, but I will not be there.'

'I will tell her more than that.' His voice was stern. 'This whole thing has got out of hand. You will hear no more of it, I promise.'

'I will not be around to hear more. I expect to receive a reply from Malmesbury at any moment and will start on my journey immediately.'

She turned on her heels and was marching towards the door when Gabriel's voice called after her. 'You cannot really mean to go as a governess.'

She swung round, her expression still fiery. 'Naturally my new position will lack the glory of a husband bought by Claremont money, but I will be well compensated by the pride of working for my living.'

'Think, Elinor! You are nobly born – and not just on

the Claremont side. You cannot spend your life drudging in some humble home.'

'Humble maybe, but blessedly free from humiliation.' She resumed her march towards the open doorway saying in a clear, cold voice, 'I wish to be private until I leave. Pray allow me that indulgence.' With a sharp snap, the door shut behind her.

Gabriel grabbed the decanter and poured himself another brandy. He needed a second drink and probably a third and a fourth. Of late he'd rarely felt the impulse, but now he decided he would make a night of it. He did not want Elinor to marry a Mr Ferrers; he did not want her to marry anyone. How could she believe him to be so crass as to plot such a thing with his aunt? He was incensed with her and incensed with Celia. Ever since the truth of Elinor's birth had become known, his aunt had been hinting at her departure from Amersham. Perhaps she feared the long dead scandal would be reborn with all its shameful repercussions; perhaps she still held her elder brother in respect and Elinor was a constant reproach to her image of the dead man. Whatever the reason, it seemed that she had decided the girl should leave and very soon.

He drained his glass and sank further into the chair's ample depths, a morose expression darkening his handsome features. For once he had tried to do the right thing. Elinor had come crashing into his world and turned it upside down. He had tried to accept the startling discovery of her parentage with equanimity. God knows, his family was nothing to be proud of, dukes though they may be. He had wanted to accept her into Amersham and then forget her. Instead she'd been a perpetual thorn in his flesh: always finding fault, always reminding him of her damn independence, always there – warm, inviting, delectable. He should have sent her packing from the moment she started poking around the house. He should have seen it could only mean trouble if she stayed. She was a constant disturbance, a constant temptation, and he longed to find peace in his mind and his body. Now it seemed he would get his wish. She was leaving, leaving in anger, and she would never return. A light went out somewhere in his heart and he reached for the decanter.

Chapter Eighteen

When Alice came to prepare her lady for bed she brought with her a worrying tale of Gabriel's excess. It was clear the duke intended to drink himself under the table, the maid whispered. It was brandy too. Brandy was wicked, Alice said knowledgeably, even the best French stuff. It rotted your guts and addled your brain. Judging by the volley of bad-tempered curses issuing from the duke, the brain addling had not yet progressed far, but no good could come of such a bad situation. The duke's man had given up trying to reason with his master and the household was holding its breath for the mischief to come.

Elinor dismissed her maid as soon as she could. She heard Alice's footsteps retreating down the tower steps and climbed from her bed. The household had retired early tonight and she knew that sleep would not come easily. She drew back the curtains and looked out at the encircling dark. A shaft of moonlight had emerged faintly from behind clouds and was slowly cutting a swathe through trees and lawn. She had listened to Alice's recital with dismay and a little guilt since she knew she had let rage overcome her and make her unfair. But the thought of Gabriel having any part in the search for an accommodating husband was humiliating. Humiliating, too, that she was considered only good enough to marry an *arriviste* who doubtless had more money than manners. The sentiment shocked her – she had become as arrogant as the Claremonts. If that is what association with the duke and his clan had done, the sooner she was on her way the better. And if Gabriel chose to drink himself into a stupor, so be it.

~

Two floors below the duke was doing his best to comply. It wouldn't be the first time. There were months after his brother had been killed that he drank himself insensible every night, alone and furious at anyone who tried to intervene. But he had come through and lately he had even begun to think the future might offer a chink of light. A mistake. If Elinor left he would return to his old life, to the same dreary, inevitable round.

He understood her indignation. How could she not be angry at being coupled with this Ferrers – the man was a pygmy – but in truth her anger came from elsewhere, though she refused to see it. It was rooted in the mawkish vision of love she clung to. Marriage was a contract, a business like any other, but she refused to see the reality and entertained foolish dreams of an all-consuming passion. She painted the attachment between her mother and his hated uncle as a hopeless romance. That was a milk-and-water tale he declined to swallow. It reminded him too much of his own parents' story. Their rose-tinted vision had left him and his brother orphans. That was the destructive power of love that Elinor refused to accept.

He brooded on the iniquity as evening turned to night and tumbler followed tumbler.

As the hours wore on his drinking slowed, but he had eaten nothing and his stomach was in a constant quarrel with his head. He felt aggrieved that he should feel so wretched. Irate, too. What right had Elinor Milford to take him to task? He had done nothing since he'd known she was his cousin but make life easier for her. She had no right to castigate him and he was going to set the record straight. She had assumed the worst of him, assumed he was behind his aunt's vulgar plotting. She had more or less accused him of selling her into marriage. He would make her apologise for flinging such base accusations at him. They were as false as she. He wanted some recompense for the trouble she had caused. He wanted her to say she was sorry. By midnight he had worked himself into a towering fury.

The huge ormolu clock in the Great Hall struck twelve. She would be abed by now, too late to have it out with her. Or was it? Visiting her bedchamber at this time of night might scare her. Did he care? No, he decided, he did not. She deserved to be scared. He walked up the tower steps, hardly missing a stair, and banged loudly on Elinor's door, arousing much of the household in the process if he had but known it. There was no response so he banged louder.

This time he heard footsteps moving lightly in his direction and the door was opened a few inches. Her eyes looked dark in the candlelight and her hair was braided over her shoulders. He saw through the crack that she was wearing a low cut nightgown whose lace clung lovingly to her breasts and that her face was flushed from sleep.

'Your Grace?' she said uncertainly. 'It must be past midnight.'

'I'm well aware of the time, Miss Milford.' He didn't so much as slur a word. 'I need to speak to you.'

'But surely it can wait until the morning.'

'It cannot,' and he pushed the door forcibly inwards. She staggered back and clutched the back of a chair for support. 'Whatever is it? What has happened?'

'You have happened,' and his words now were beginning to lose a little of their clarity. 'You!' and he pointed dramatically at her. Her expression was confused, wavering between alarm and amusement.

'You have infiltrated my kingdom,' he said grandiosely. 'Infiltrated, like a spy, poked around my home and upset my household.'

She tried to reason with him. 'You must know I am no spy. If I have indeed caused upset to your household, I am truly sorry.'

Reason was not going to be Gabriel's strong suit that night. 'It's me you owe an apology to. I accepted you into my home, a gentlemanly courtesy that I regret. Because I *am* a gentleman, no matter what kind of rascally relatives I'm burdened with.' Then in a low mutter, 'I should have turned you from the door.'

'There is no need for these histrionics,' she said crisply. 'I am leaving in two days. A message arrived late this evening, a gratifying response from the lady in Wiltshire. So you see, there is nothing to fret you.'

She moved towards him in an attempt to push him back through the open door, but infuriated by her seemingly patronizing words, he grabbed at her.

'Fret, fret? I have done nothing but fret. I have not had one comfortable moment since you arrived. I intend that you pay for my discomfort.'

His arms wrapped her around, his hands burning through the fine silk of her nightdress to leave an imprint of desire. His face hovered close, then his mouth was on hers and he was kissing her hungrily. She tasted the brandy on his lips, tasted the urgent warmth of his touch. He reached for her braid and in a moment had released her hair and lost his fingers in its tangle of curls. His kisses forced her mouth open and she made no protest. Slowly he drew her tongue into his mouth and caressed it with his own, all the while holding her body against his hardening form. She could not have escaped if she had wanted to.

And she didn't. His lips withdrew from hers leaving her mouth bruised and yearning, but now they were moving down her neck in small butterfly kisses that plunged ever lower until he reached her breasts. A throbbing ache of pleasure shot through her. He was pushing her towards the bed and she was letting him when a sharp voice sounded from the doorway.

'Gabriel! Your Grace! You forget yourself.'

It was Celia. He turned swiftly and Elinor's nightgown fell modestly back into place. 'Go to bed,' he commanded his aunt.

'Indeed I will not. You are drunk and threatening an innocent girl with your wickedness. I will not sleep another night beneath such an impure roof. And neither will Elinor.'

His eyes looked suddenly alert. He looked around the room and then at Elinor as though he could not believe where he was. Lady Frant took advantage of this unexpected docility and steered him towards the stairway. 'Your Grace needs to return to your own room.' He went without another word.

Celia turned to her charge. 'Why did you not call for help?' she demanded suspiciously. 'How could you have allowed him to place you in such a compromising situation?'

Elinor breathed an inner sigh of relief. Gabriel had had his back to the door shielding her from the sight of anyone coming into the room. His aunt could not have witnessed the full immodesty of their conduct.

'I did not think I was in danger,' she prevaricated.

'Did you not?' Celia's tone was disbelieving. She dragged a valise from beneath the bed and proceeded to open the drawers of the large chest that filled one corner of the room.

'What are you doing?'

'What it is necessary to do. I am taking you to live at the Dower House where you will be safe from further assault.'

'There is no need, Lady Frant. The duke was not himself. I am sure he will not repeat such behaviour and I will be leaving Amersham in two days.'

Celia looked gratified. 'Nevertheless it will be a great deal safer if you spend those days away from the Hall. Gabriel is too frequently not himself.'

Elinor was trembling with the aftermath of the encounter and too exhausted to argue. The duke's initial hostility had surprised and upset her. That first kiss had been angry, almost as though he were intent on exacting recompense.

But the anger had melted along with the kiss and instead she had felt a hard, sweet searching of her lips. She had opened her mouth to accept him, opened her body to his touch. She had been reduced to a mass of sensation, desperate to feed her spiralling desire. Only Celia's arrival on the scene had stopped their mutual seduction. The older woman was right. It was dangerous to stay at the Hall, even more dangerous than Lady Frant knew, for it was not just the duke who could not be trusted. She could no longer trust herself.

❧

Roland arrived at the Dower House from a convivial evening in Steyning at the same time as his mother and Elinor dragged a large valise through the front door.

'What on earth...'

'Miss Milford is staying with us until she leaves for Malmesbury.' His mother's tone brooked no argument.

'But -'

'It is quite settled.' She turned to the young woman. 'Let me take you to your bedchamber. The maid can unpack for you tomorrow.' An unprotesting Elinor was led up the stairs to one of the small rooms at the very top of the house.

When Celia Frant returned to the drawing room, her son was moodily kicking at a dying log in the hearth. 'This is all very well, Mama, but think of the gossip your flight from the Hall must occasion. And leaving at this time of night! It would surely have been more discreet to have asked a servant to bring the luggage on later.'

His mother looked at him witheringly. 'Unfortunately your louche cousin is unacquainted with discretion. By now the whole household will have been alerted to the shocking incident.'

'Whatever has Gabriel done?'

'The details are unnecessary,' she said tight-lipped. 'It is sufficient for you to know that Elinor Milford will remain in this house until she leaves for Wiltshire.'

'But what about Mr Ferrers?'

'Mr Ferrers will marry elsewhere. My efforts have gone unappreciated and Miss Milford intends to take up a teaching post. I no longer care what she does as long as she goes from here, but in the meantime she will stay with us.'

'Are you sure you can trust me with her?' he asked sulkily.

'I never for one moment doubted that I could.'

Roland's face expressed disbelief and keen to irritate his mother, he decided on the most annoying question he could think of. 'So what happens to your plan of obtaining a foothold at the Hall?'

Celia smiled serenely. 'I have already done so. I have been living there nigh on three weeks and tonight I have rescued Gabriel from the likely embarrassment of a drunken misdemeanour. He will be grateful, you will see. We must be sure to keep the girl from him until we can put her on the stage at Steyning. There must be no further complications.'

Roland did not share his mother's confidence that a splendid future was close at hand, but he knew better than to voice his doubts. He shrugged his shoulders and went to bed.

Chapter Nineteen

Gabriel groaned and turned over. Then groaned again. The sliver of light escaping into the room through drawn curtains made him snap his eyes shut in pain. Summers stood silently by his bedside proffering a glass of peppermint water. 'May I suggest that Your Grace drink this?'

'You may suggest all you like. Then just go away,' Gabriel said thickly.

'Your Grace may wish to know that Mr Henderson has called.'

'Who?'

'Mr Joffey's assistant.'

He remembered vaguely they'd had an appointment. Something to do with a bridge.

'And?'

'Mr Henderson waited for an hour and then had to leave. He had urgent business on the Home Farm.'

The valet could not have accused him more directly of wasting his subordinate's time and leaving his own duties unattended.

'Damn you, Summers,' he said resignedly. 'Give me the

wretched glass.' He drank it in one swallow and shuddered. 'It had better work or you'll be looking for a new situation.'

He saw the slight smile creasing his valet's face. The man had been his batman when both had served in the 14th Light Dragoons and before that his boyhood attendant at Amersham. Summers knew him better than anyone alive.

'What will Your Grace wear?'

He had no interest in his dress. He had no interest in leaving his bed. He remembered sufficient of his last night's conduct to know his day would be one of unmitigated grovelling.

'Anything. No. Wait. Something sober, modest, but I don't want to look like a damn Quaker. *She* does that too well,' he muttered.

Summers affected not to hear this last comment and carefully laid out fawn pantaloons, a coat of dark blue superfine and the one indulgence, a waistcoat of white satin embroidered with small blue flowers. If he judged the occasion right, his master would need to present himself a polished man. The duke meanwhile remained prone, shielding his eyes from the small amount of light in the room and wondering if he would ever manage to rise.

In thirty minutes he was discussing a surprisingly substantial breakfast. Three cups of coffee and he was feeling a good deal better, except for what lay ahead. He would have to walk to the Dower House and apologise. There was no help for it. Last night she had spurred him to such passion he had made a complete fool of himself. And now he was about to make a fool of himself again. But there was no way out of it, he would have to apologise. She was leaving in two days, wasn't that what she'd said? Surely he could play the gentleman until he saw her safely dispatched to Wiltshire.

He didn't want her in Wiltshire, didn't want her living unesteemed, her soul sapped for a pittance, her looks and health lost to the slavery that was governessing. But what was the alternative for a girl too high born to be a servant but too poor for the world in which she truly belonged? A girl who had rejected the smallest hint of monetary help with a formidable anger. There was no alternative. Only marriage. Celia Frant had been right about that at least. It had to be marriage. No matter how much she might protest, Elinor needed a husband. But not Mr Ferrers, he thought. What must his aunt have been thinking? Not Mr Ferrers, nor anyone like him. Elinor was a lady, beautiful and intelligent. She deserved the very best. But who? No one worthy came to mind.

He sat staring at his devilled kidneys for nearly ten minutes thinking hard. Then it came to him. She could marry him! He would offer himself as her husband – cousins could marry. She belonged at Amersham and if they married, she could stay at the Hall for ever. She loved the house and it was right she should make it her home. And as for him, he must one day marry and provide an heir. He had been assiduous in pushing that thought away, just as he had pushed away knowledge of Jonathan's death. If Jonty had lived, his brother would have chosen a wife and secured the future of the estate. Now it was up to him. He had no heir other than Roland and the thought of his cousin becoming duke filled him with repugnance. The man was second rate, third rate even, and he would do anything to prevent him inheriting. Marriage and an heir would effectively shatter whatever ambitions Roland might be nursing.

It would be a business arrangement, he decided. He might lust after Elinor, but he did not love her. He did not love any woman, he was incapable of it, and it would be unfair to pretend otherwise. Elinor might treasure a romantic vision of love, but her history showed her to be a practical woman, certainly one who had known the hardships of life. Might she not be content with what he had to offer?

He knew her for a lively companion, someone with whom he could enjoy banter, books, the small comedies of life. And she fascinated him. He was infatuated with her – witness last night's humiliation – but in time, like all infatuations, it would burn itself out. He smiled ruefully as he remembered the way he had stormed into her room and then... he couldn't recall their lovemaking in detail, but he knew he had enjoyed every minute. She had, too. She would be a willing partner in bed and keep him interested, at least until an heir had come into the world. Then they could go their separate ways as long as they were both discreet. He would not interfere in her private friendships and would expect the same consideration. In public they would remain a devoted couple, the Duke and Duchess of Amersham. It was perfect.

⤳

Elinor breakfasted alone. Both Celia and her son had

disappeared on errands and she had time to sit quietly and ponder the events of the previous evening. Too much time. They had now begun to assume hideous proportions. She had not only failed to raise the alarm as soon as Gabriel blundered into her room, but had allowed him the most appalling freedom. He was drunk, it was true, and he was a large man, but he had not forced her. She had wanted his touch, longed for it to continue. Even now she could feel her body sing. She had always suspected that staying at Amersham would prove perilous and now she had its full measure. The memory of their bodies so closely entwined would be with her for years – but it had to remain a memory.

She must stay sequestered within the Dower House until Monday when Roland's carriage would take her to the White Horse and the London-bound coach for the first stage of her journey to Malmesbury. She would breathe more easily then, she told herself. She looked up as she heard a crunch of gravel outside the breakfast room and saw through the window a tall figure advancing towards the front door. She was not going to breathe easily after all.

Lady Frant's maid announced the duke, her eyes fairly goggling. It was clear that news of the night's disturbance had travelled around the Hall and beyond. How very dreadful! Gabriel strode through the open doorway and she saw with surprise he was dressed as though for a formal occasion. A slight flush warmed his tanned skin, but he betrayed no awkwardness as he came forward to make his bow.

'Good morning, cousin,' he said deliberately. He rarely

called her that and she could see it was for the maid's benefit.

'It is a beautiful morning and I wondered if I might interest you in a stroll. The gardens are looking particularly fine.'

She was going to refuse but then saw the appeal on his face and the maid's fascinated stare. This was better than a play for her and Elinor could see she was storing up every minute to recount to her fellows later in the day.

'I will fetch my bonnet,' she said hurriedly.

Once in her room she cast around for the plainest she owned, but ended cramming on her head the only hat in sight, a charming high-brimmed confection fashioned from *broderie anglaise* and trimmed with cream flowers. She hoped he would not feel the need to offer her compliments on it, but when she rejoined him in the breakfast room he said nothing and ushered her directly into the hall and through the front door, leaving the maid paralysed with mouth ajar.

⌒

They walked slowly across the sloping lawns. The hour was still early and the sun gentle. The clustered perfume of roses wafted towards them from the nearby arbour and a flight of swallows arrowed the sky above. At any other time they would have delighted in such a morning. Along a series of steps, terrace by terrace they strolled, dropping downwards through a network of gravelled paths towards the smooth oval of the lake.

There had been silence between them until the duke said quietly, 'Thank you for agreeing to walk with me this morning.' She said nothing but continued at a steady pace.

'Thank you,' he repeated. 'It was important I see you. I need to apologise for my conduct last night. I am sincerely sorry.'

When she still said nothing he was moved to add, 'You must know that I was not quite myself.'

'I may have led a sheltered life,' she retorted, 'but I can recognise when a man is – what is the expression – half-sprung.'

'Then I hope you will forget my temporary lapse of good manners.'

'I would be more than happy to forget what can only be a painful memory for us both.'

Not so painful, he thought, remembering the warmth of her mouth and the way her body had melted against his. It was a very sweet memory, but he was not about to share it. He had business to conduct and said in what he hoped was a neutral voice, 'I was unreasonably angry with you – for accusing me unjustly. And for being so determined to leave Amersham for a job that cannot be anything but thankless.'

'Have we not had this conversation before?'

'I am attempting to explain why I behaved so badly.'

'I thought we had just agreed we would not think further on it.'

By now they had walked a good distance from the Dower House and a large expanse of water shimmered before them, shadowed on all sides by willow trees which lovingly bent to kiss its surface.

'We have reached the lake and I should be returning,'

she said, 'else Lady Frant will wonder where I am.'

'Before you do, let's walk across the bridge while we have the chance. It is unlikely to survive for much longer.'

An island had been built at the very centre of the lake and from there a fountain played continuously, sending concentric ripples lapping softly at its edge. Several schools of fish foraged in the clear waters or played amid its waving weeds. He watched as Elinor walked half way along the wooden structure and leant over its worn parapet to gaze at the smallest fish as they darted for cover.

For once he found himself at a loss for words and when he joined her on the bridge, it was to say hesitantly, 'I have thought much about our mutual situation.'

She offered no help, staring at him in puzzlement, and he realised this interview was going to be far more difficult than he had imagined.

'I need to marry,' he said bluntly. 'I am the only surviving Claremont and who knows, I could go into a decline at any time.'

The joke went unacknowledged and she continued to look questioningly at him. 'There is the delicate business of an heir, you see,' he said awkwardly. 'I will have to marry.'

'But you have an heir – your cousin?'

'An heir who is his father's son, a true Frant. What he is not is a Claremont, but *you* are. In all but name. I hope you will agree to take that as your own. Rightfully it belongs to you.'

Her face manifested utter bewilderment. He was making a complete mull of it. The man who could twist women around his finger and get whatever he wanted. In desperation, he blurted out, 'I hope you will accept my offer of marriage.'

'What!'

'I am asking you to marry me, Elinor.'

She stood stock still and looked directly at him. Her eyes were at the level of his chin and her glance did not waver. 'Are you newly drunk or is this the aftermath of last night's indulgence?'

'It is neither. It is a serious proposition. Please listen to what I have to say before you reject the idea. I think it will work admirably for both of us.'

'Work? Are we talking of marriage or a business undertaking?'

This was the opening he had hoped for. 'It is both. That is the beauty of my scheme. *I* must marry; I must have an heir. *You* are in need of a home and where more appropriate than Amersham? I know that you will say you have found employment, that you have no need of a husband. But think of the years to come. Will you still feel similarly as a much older woman?'

He was now in full flow, his confidence restored. It really was that simple and surely she would see the benefits for them both. But she was staring fixedly, not at him, but somewhere far into the distance. When she spoke, her voice was dazed, a little flat. 'So this is to be a marriage of convenience?'

'I would not pretend otherwise and you are too honest not to agree. We may not be in love, but neither are we romantically involved with others. There would seem to be no impediment to our marrying.'

He allowed his words to percolate before continuing, 'You may feel it too much a business arrangement and I understand your scruples, but don't reject the idea for that reason. Rather think of it as coming home. You will live at Amersham Hall where you always should have done. Your mother would rightly have been mistress here and now you will reign in her place. As for me, I could not choose a better partner to share the running of the estate.'

He talked on in this vein for some minutes while Elinor remained silent. She was stunned. The man seemed in earnest. He was offering her a wedding ring! And not just any wedding ring. If she accepted she would be the Duchess of Amersham. It was absurd. She would be mistress of this beautiful property – its gardens, woods, pastures, streams – and that wasn't quite so absurd. But how could she ever agree to such a ridiculous proposal? He had denied that he was in any way out of control. His mind was certainly logical – he'd given her some very good reasons why such a marriage might work – but still, he could not really be in earnest. Tomorrow he would return shamefaced asking her to forgive another temporary lapse of good sense.

Aloud she said, 'I will consider your proposition, Gabriel.' She could not bring herself to call it a proposal. 'And give you my answer tomorrow.'

He looked relieved that a difficult conversation was over. 'With your permission I will wait on you in the morning – at ten o'clock, if that is convenient.'

'Perfectly,' she said briskly. 'Now I must leave you.'

Chapter Twenty

She retraced her steps to the Dower House, still unconvinced the duke was truly sincere, but with the corners of her mind beginning to flirt very slightly with the idea. It was lucky that Celia Frant and her son continued absent for much of the day. They would certainly have noticed something amiss and she had no wish to alert them to what had happened. In case the duke was as good as his word and was tomorrow knocking at her door, she needed time alone to work out what her reply should be. But if, as she suspected, he thought better of his impulse, the Frants need never know she had received any such proposition.

And what a proposition. Gabriel had presented it as a business arrangement and she could understand why. He was highly attracted to her, she knew, infatuated even, but he did not love her. Except for his brother, he seemed to have loved no one, and when Jonathan died on the battlefield what love Gabriel possessed had died with him. It made sense, therefore, that he marry without emotion, and sense that by doing so he could recompense an illegitimate child for the slights and privations of the past.

But did it make sense for her? Her heart sang whenever she saw his tall figure saunter through the courtyard or sit carelessly astride his chestnut mare. She loved the smile he could not repress even when he was berating her, and the deep blue eyes at times so tender. Last night she had craved his touch. Feeling this intensely, was it wise to enter into a marriage of convenience with a man who could stir her so? She doubted she would ever be able to light the same flame in him. She had made him burn last night. He had been fuddled, but not so fuddled he had not known what he was doing and not so fuddled he had not enjoyed every second of it.

But that was a simple physical connection. What if she wanted more? She would be a fool if she did. Long ago she had recognised she was destined for a single life. Her face and figure might commend her, but without a dowry she was never likely to attract a serious suitor. Men had always been eager to flirt with her, but just as eager to steer clear of commitment. She'd had no illusions about finding a husband, and then out of the blue one had presented himself. And what a husband. If she married Gabriel, she would never have to look for the next penny, never have to face an unwilling pupil. Never have to churn a bowl of milk or pat a block of butter into shape. Instead her life would be one of luxury.

As her mother's should have been. If only Charles Claremont had shown courage, he would have defied his father and married where he loved, and Grainne would have been Duchess of Amersham. Was it possible that as the daughter of their tragic union she might assume the title in her mother's stead? Madame Demelza's prophecy came dramatically to mind. Is that what she had meant? That she, Elinor, would save the woman the clairvoyant had seen, the woman from over the sea, the dark haired woman in distress. She would save her and make all right. By becoming the duchess, by making Amersham her home, would she bring her mother final peace? The thought caught in her throat and would not be dislodged.

∽

The duke presented himself at the Dower House on the dot of ten o'clock the next morning. Summers had again exerted himself and his master was looking precise to a pin in dove grey stirrup trousers, a striped silk waistcoat and a neckcloth tied in a perfect Waterfall. Although Roland had ridden away after breakfast, Celia Frant was at home and looked astonished as her nephew's fashionable form crossed her threshold.

'I thought we had agreed you would not venture here until Miss Milford had departed,' she greeted him crossly.

He ignored his aunt, looking over her head at the figure of Elinor walking towards him along the carpeted passageway.

'Well?' he enquired as she arrived, a slight smile lighting his face. Evidently he had not changed his mind.

Lady Frant looked from one to the other, baffled.

Elinor took a deep breath. 'I am happy to agree to your proposition,' she said.

∽

The ceremony was to take place in the family chapel within the fortnight and only the bride and groom with their two witnesses would be present. Celia had remembered an urgent engagement with a distant friend in East Anglia and Roland had been bullied into accompanying her, to protect the coach should she meet with any stray highwaymen. Both bride and groom were delighted. Gabriel was well aware of his aunt's ill feeling while Elinor had no wish to stand at the altar with what remained of his family glowering from the pews. In the meantime she was left alone at the Dower House with Alice as her chief companion. The duke had been adamant they should not live under the same roof until the knot was tied. He had heard several scurrilous tales already circulating in the neighbourhood and wanted to save her as far as possible from further scandal.

The days leading up to the wedding should have been joyous. Instead she felt miserably fatigued, for at night she was sleeping badly and during the day she found it impossible to settle. She needed always to be on the move and since she wished only for her own company, she kept to the Dower House garden. Every day she walked its winding pathways, hollyhocks still resplendent in their summer colours standing sentinel on either side. Round and round she walked, her mind circling in unison. She could not still the tiresome refrain that played incessantly in her head. Was she making a sensible marriage of convenience or taking a foolish gamble on a pair of deep blue eyes?

Her walk today was in hot sun, an Indian summer in the offing it seemed, and for once she paused to rest. She had reached the bower at the centre of the garden and sank gratefully down on its sun-warmed bench. The heavy perfume of roses crowded in on her. In her calmer moments she could pretend her emotions were under control, that she was marrying for practical reasons or marrying where her mother had failed, but today as she sat, eyelids closed to the embrace of sunlight, she was forced to acknowledge the truth. It wasn't so. She had fallen entirely under Gabriel's spell and she was marrying not for her mother's sake nor to secure a home. She was marrying because she loved him. It was a confession she longed to shout aloud, to shout from the rooftops – except that *he* had no such confession to make. He would stand at the altar for a very different reason. She might be marrying with her heart, but he was marrying with his head.

Two days before the wedding a footman from the Hall presented himself at the door with one very large box and several smaller packages. Alice called excitedly to her mistress since she had a strong inkling of what these fascinating parcels might contain.

'You must come, miss. There are boxes to open.'

Elinor walked slowly through the door and stared. 'But where have these come from?'

'Thomas brought them. From the Hall,' Alice added, seeing her mistress's puzzled expression.

When Elinor continued to stare at the laden table, the maid did a little jig of impatience. 'Do open 'em, Miss Elinor,' she urged.

'Why don't you open them for me?'

Alice needed no second bidding. In a trice she had ripped apart the smaller packages and drawn forth a shawl of spider gauze, white satin slippers decorated with silver roses, a silver threaded reticule and the wickedest confection of silver net.

'Is that really a hat?' Elinor's eyes were wide with amazement.

'It is, miss, and the most beautiful hat I've ever seen.' And Alice waltzed around the kitchen holding the fragile construction in both hands as though it were her partner in a dance. 'Isn't it wonderful?' she breathed.

'Wonderful,' Elinor said uncertainly.

If the small parcels contained such riches, what would she find in the large box that filled the entire table top? She was not long in discovering since her maid had set upon the parcel with vigour. The lid was off, the tissue crumpled, and two faces peered into its depths.

'Oh, my goodness,' Elinor said.

'Oh, my goodness,' Alice echoed, reverently drawing the exquisite gown from its nest and smoothing down its folds as she did.

Elinor looked at her wedding dress held aloft in her maid's arms and caught her breath. It was of figured white silk with an overdress of spangled silver gauze and she knew just by looking that it would mould and curve itself around her form to perfection. So much beauty – but so little love.

It could have been a moment to weep. Instead she said briskly, 'We will need to hang it carefully if it's to be without a crease on Friday.'

⌒

By half past eleven on Friday morning, she was dressed in the finery Gabriel had chosen. Colour and fit were perfect and when she looked in the mirror, a fairy princess looked back. But this was not a fairy tale, it was reality; a sensible decision, a rational arrangement between relatives, she told herself sternly. At a quarter to noon, a knock on the door heralded her bridegroom. He came alone and he was beautiful. Light-coloured satin breeches, a black coat fitting tightly across his shoulders and a frilled shirt, dazzlingly white, filled her vision. One single diamond held the intricate folds of a pure white linen cravat.

He offered her his arm and together they began the walk along the broad gravel drive leading to the house. Although they spoke little, he was intent on putting her at her ease and she felt grateful. A short distance and they branched off from the main carriage way and followed a narrower, flagged path to the chapel, drawing ever nearer to the sound of carolling bells. The church sat within a cluster of silver birch and once they had broached the circle of trees, she could see Mr Jarvis and Mrs Lucas awaiting them. The two upper servants came forward to pay their respects and followed them into the dim light of the chapel to kneel before the parson. The ceremony was simple and in ten minutes they were wed.

An equally simple wedding breakfast followed, shared only by the newly-weds, the parson quick to excuse himself from this unusual ceremony. Elinor picked lightly at her food. She had not eaten that day, but was finding it difficult to swallow even the smallest of dainties Cook had created for the occasion. Now that the deed was done, she should surely be able to cast aside the doubts that had plagued her. But new doubts had taken their place; she could not stop herself thinking of what lay ahead that night.

They were not the worries of most virgin brides. If

Gabriel had loved her, this would be the finest day of her life and she would have longed for darkness to fall and for them to be alone at last. But he did not love her and she must never allow him to see her true feelings. He would expect his bride to be willing, even perhaps passionate, but he would not expect profound emotion. That would challenge their very agreement. And what if she disappointed him in the night ahead? She had no experience other than his stolen kisses, while he had known many women, women who had every trick of lovemaking at their fingertips.

It was still early in the afternoon when the duke asked for his curricle to be brought to the door. She was glad he had thought to fill the next few hours by tooling his new wife around the estate, occasionally getting down from the carriage to introduce particular tenants. She guessed a good deal of lively gossip had circulated in the neighbourhood once the duke's intention to wed had become known and he would be keen to scotch some of the wilder surmises.

As they drove she felt him snatching quick glances at her, seeming unsure whether to speak or not. And when he did, it was to warn her of the possible consequences of their hasty wedding.

'I'm afraid we are likely to be the subject of much talk for months to come.' He gave her hand a comforting squeeze.

'I would imagine you are not a stranger to gossip,' she returned.

'I am concerned not for myself, but for you.'

'You are very thoughtful, but I am well able to look after myself.' She sat erect, chin raised proudly.

'You will hear things that anger you.'

'That I have not a feather to fly with and am a shameless fortune hunter?'

'I think that may be an accusation, but also...' He seemed uncertain how to continue.

'Also...'

'Also – there will be those who say it must have been necessary for us to marry.'

She flushed. 'I daresay. No doubt my mother provoked similar talk, but the gossips will find me in very different case.'

He said no more on the subject and they continued to while away the afternoon before a slow return to the great house. As they approached the Hall, she noticed how verdant the grass remained on either side of the carriage way, while in the distance the trees were beginning to lose their rich covering. Autumn was around the corner and she felt strangely melancholy.

'I intended to drive over to Brighton after our wedding,' Gabriel was saying, 'and personally break the news of our marriage to the Regent. But I believe George has already abandoned his seaside haunt for Carlton House. We will have no alternative but to visit London and confess!'

'How will he take it, do you think?'

'Much like everyone else, I imagine.' He grimaced. 'He will think I have finally lost my senses. Then when he is in despair, I shall produce you. He will remember how beautiful you are and realise I have been guilty only of exercising the greatest of taste.'

To know that Gabriel was charmed by her was precious, but she had no wish to visit London and certainly no wish ever to see his erstwhile companions again. Her acquaintance with them was already more than sufficient.

As though sensing the direction of her thoughts, he said, 'You must not think I intend to be a great deal in London, unless you wish it. There is much to do at Amersham – I've known that ever since I came home – but now I intend to work so hard that Joffey will be hard pressed to keep up with me!'

The curricle had come to a halt at the great front door and for a moment both its passengers stayed quite still, taken aback by what awaited them. Two lines of servants were drawn up facing each other, every one of them dressed in their very best clothes and the women holding small posies of flowers. As Gabriel took his bride's arm and walked her through the arch of well-wishers, they began a loud clapping.

Elinor turned pink with pleasure. She was touched by the evident goodwill and walked slowly between the two lines, her face glowing. Smiling to left and right, she accepted the flowers the women offered until Gabriel could hardly see her for bouquets. Mrs Lucas and a maid relieved her of the posies and promised the flowers would shortly reappear to decorate her apartments. As a mark of her new status, she had been moved to the blue bedroom situated over the main entrance and with her own sitting room attached.

The housekeeper proudly led the way. 'For you will be wanting a little rest, I'm sure, Your Grace, before dinner.'

Elinor was startled. The title seemed wholly unreal, but seeing the housekeeper's enquiring face she managed to inspect the room and smile her approval. 'It is quite beautiful, Mrs. Lucas. Thank you for choosing it.'

'His Grace did that. Only the very best for Miss Milford, he said.'

Elinor walked through the sitting room into the bedroom, the housekeeper following. The bed was huge and the view over the stately drive and the distant woods magnificent. She could have asked for no better.

'Where does that lead, Mrs Lucas?' She pointed to a small door built into the far wall.

'That is His Grace's bedroom,' the housekeeper answered, her eyes not quite meeting Elinor's.

'Of course,' she said, her voice faltering a little.

'Will that be all, Your Grace?' The housekeeper's voice was unusually gentle. It made Elinor wonder if the servants were aware of the nature of her marriage.

'Yes, thank you, Mrs Lucas. The rooms are splendid.'

Chapter Twenty-One

By the time she glided down the stairs that evening, her hair and gown as near perfect as Alice could ensure, the duke was waiting for her in the drawing room. It was still early September but already the nights were closing in and a fire had been lit to ward off the chill. As she walked through the door he held a glass of wine out to her, but then his hand appeared to stop mid-air. He was staring hard and she wondered if it was the emerald gown she wore, cut low across the bosom, that had surprised him. Or perhaps the glow she felt in every part of her body had sparked an awareness in him. Whatever it was, for an instant he appeared mesmerised, then he was kissing her lightly on the cheek and ushering her towards the fire.

The dinner Cook had prepared was light and tempting: a *consommé* followed by turbot with shrimp sauce, then roast fillet of beef and *poulets à la rèine* served with Lyonnaise potatoes and green beans, and to finish a Parisian meringue and apple soufflé. Each dish was garnished with rose petals and served on fine floral china. But once again both ate sparingly.

Dinner was over and tea brought to the drawing room.

The servants evidently expected an early bedtime. Conversation became desultory and at ten o'clock Gabriel returned his cup and saucer to the tea tray and rose to his feet.

'I imagine you will wish to retire now.' His tone was oddly bright. 'But I will join you very shortly.'

She wondered if he were nervous. His voice suggested he might be, but she dismissed the thought even as it arose. If he *were* nervous, it was for her alone. He was sensitive enough to imagine the ordeal she was facing, but his imaginings would not come close to the reality. He could not know what she really feared.

Alice undressed her reverently. A new silk and lace nightgown, recently delivered by one of London's finest modistes, lay ready on the bed. Elinor's dark curls were brushed to a shining cloud and the diamonds that winked in her ears placed in a drawer for safekeeping. The lights were shuttered until only one candle remained. The scene was set and Alice closed the door quietly behind her. All Elinor had to do was lie and wait.

Gabriel walked to the dresser and snuffed out the one candle, then to the window to draw back the curtains. The moon rode clear from behind drifting rags of cloud and shone brightly into the room, silvering its contents and making Elinor feel she had entered a strange and exotic world. His night shirt fell to the floor and she had a brief glimpse of his strong male form before he slipped between the covers and was there beside her, his skin warming hers. She lay immobile, frozen with longing and with dread. She must play the counterfeit; she dared not show him the truth of her feelings, the deep emotions which lay in ambush.

A quiet voice sounded in her ear. 'The night is chilly and we must keep each other warm,' and he tugged gently at her nightgown, inching it upwards until he had slipped it over her head and cast it adrift.

He turned towards her, leaning on one arm, and smoothed back the dark halo of hair spread across the pillow. His index finger traced a line down her cheek.

'There is something I wish to say, Elinor. We have made a marriage of convenience, but it does not mean we cannot be considerate of each other. Your happiness must be mine.'

'Thank you,' she murmured, touched by his concern.

Then his arms were encircling her and pulling her close. The heat from his body flooded through every fibre and his musky scent filled the air she breathed. She was dizzy with his nearness and felt herself falling, falling. Small kisses plucked at her hair and nuzzled at her ears. Then his lips were gently pulling at hers; gently at first but then more strongly, more insistently. Her stomach clenched with a deep pleasure. Eagerly she opened her mouth to him until her body burned and her breathing grew ragged. His lips created a trail of delight, down her cheek, her jaw, her neck, to hover over the smooth cream of her bosom. Desperate to know his touch, she took his head between her hands and brought his mouth to her breasts, her fingers turning and twining in his dark hair. She heard herself moan as his lips continued their inexorable journey downwards and he was touching her where she had never before been touched. Every nerve in her body was ablaze. The pleasure was excruciating, but she wanted more. She could forbear no longer. She grabbed his shoulders with her hands and brought him fiercely down upon her.

'Elinor, my love.' Had she heard those words? She hardly knew. She arched into his body and let herself drown in the firestorm of passion.

⌒

Gabriel woke as the first shafts of sunlight spilled across the counterpane. For a moment he looked dazedly around the room and then remembered. His mind shut down abruptly. He inched his way to the side of the bed, careful not to disturb the woman sleeping so soundly beside him, and on tiptoe made for the connecting door to his own apartments. Summers was already there, but looked surprised to see his master so early in the morning. He made no comment, however, and went about his business in silence, fetching hot water for washing and laying out the riding dress the duke commanded.

In less than an hour Gabriel was waking the sleepy stable boy to help him saddle his favourite chestnut. All he wanted was to get away from the house, to get away and gain time to think. No, he didn't want to think – about his marriage, about Elinor, about the night. But the images kept crowding in on him. Their marriage should have been uncomplicated, a simple exchange, and this morning he should be sitting opposite her at the breakfast table smiling across the coffee cups. Instead he was galloping his mare as far and as fast as he could, escaping – but from what? He knew in his heart. It was love. He had loved her last night and it had come out of nowhere, an unwelcome intruder.

All day he had thought himself a lucky man. She was a lively companion, a sympathetic listener, and she was beautiful. He'd thought her ethereal in her wedding dress and intensely desirable in the emerald green silk she had worn to dinner. He had prepared himself for a night of pleasure, and more to come when he would savour her to the full – until his infatuation died. Or so he'd thought. Even then he had felt an edge of nervousness that should have served as a warning. But how could he have imagined that feeling would have engulfed him so ferociously?

He wanted to hold her close for ever, to sleep every night in her arms and kiss her awake every morning. He wanted to protect her from all harm, to love her with tenderness again and again. He had never before experienced such complete surrender and he hated it. Love was an enemy, fickle and untrustworthy. Those he had loved – his parents, his brother – had left him bereft. He had put his trust in them, believed they would always be there, but the world had turned and decreed otherwise. He had been left alone and he still felt the pain. Romantic love would be no different; a wife would be no different.

He looked into the future and saw darkness. He would fall deeper and deeper in love with her, he would be ecstatically happy and all would be well for a year, two years. Then she would grow discontented with her life, with him. She had not married for love after all, and there would be plenty of followers only too ready to charm the Duchess of Amersham and woo her from him. Or worse, she would die. That was not unlikely. She was a delicate creature, a fragile Celtic beauty. What would childbirth do to her? He might gain an heir, but at what cost. If he loved her, how could he ever look at his son and not despair? When you loved, it hurt. That was the lesson he had learned and he'd learned it well. He could not succumb. There was still a chance to save himself: he must separate from her, keep a distance, until such time as this wild emotion subsided. As it surely would.

He turned into one of the many rutted lanes which led back to the iron gates of Amersham. He must build a barrier of politeness between them, he decided. Elinor might be disappointed by the tepid friendship he'd offer, but she would understand their marriage was a business arrangement. She would understand its terms and not expect to live in his pocket. Last night her passion had matched his, but she had spoken no words of love. She was simply fulfilling the bargain she had made and he need not worry her emotions were deeply engaged.

He had ridden through the gates and was making his way to the stables when he became aware of a voice in the distance and looked up to see Roland Frant trotting towards him. He groaned inwardly since he had supposed his despised cousin to be safely in Norfolk.

'Good morning, Gabriel. I had not thought to see you riding so early today.'

'It's too beautiful a morning to stay abed.' He hoped his cousin's curiosity would be satisfied. 'Are you not supposed to be in Norwich still?'

'I arrived home last night. Too late for the ceremony, I regret.'

Gabriel ignored the comment and tried to turn the

conversation once more. 'And Lady Frant stays behind?'

'My mother is content enough with her old friend. They have much to talk over and I can only be in the way.' There was a trace of smugness in Roland's answer. 'I shall return to Norwich tomorrow week to escort Lady Frant home. But tell me, how is the duchess?'

'She is well.'

'And happy, I trust. This must be a most joyous day for you both. But I believe she will be happier still when she hears the news I have.'

'News?'

'I bring important tidings – but I will make an appointment to speak with her.'

'What the devil are you talking about?'

'I would not wish to disturb the newly-weds on their honeymoon,' his cousin said slyly.

'Cut to the chase, Roland. If you have something to say, say it.'

'Forgive me for prevaricating, but my news concerns the duchess most particularly.'

'Then you had better come up to the house and get it over with,' the duke said tersely.

Two hours after Gabriel had tiptoed from her bedchamber, Elinor awoke to full sunlight streaming through the window and lighting the room with its warm gold. She stretched lazily and looked to her left. He was no longer there. He must have returned to his own bed, an aristocratic custom perhaps that spared the servants their blushes. She lay for a long time gazing idly at the ceiling but seeing nothing.

Her thought was all of the night, the achingly sweet night they had passed together. With each moment relived, her smile grew wider. Why had she assumed this was going to be difficult? It had not been difficult, it had been magnificent – a tender, life-affirming night in the arms of her lover. She had known she loved him, had feared for days she would show that love too clearly. But in the end it had not mattered, for he had loved her back. He was her true sweetheart and she was his.

She stretched her hand to the bell, but before she could ring the door opened and Alice hovered on the threshold, a cup of chocolate in her hand and a jug of hot water at her feet. The maid's plump face was wreathed in smiles. She placed the chocolate on a side table and poured water into the large, white porcelain bowl.

'What will Your Grace wear today?'

Once more Elinor felt bemused. She supposed that one day she would become used to being a duchess, but really it mattered little. She was Gabriel's wife and that was all the title she needed.

'I am not sure. I don't yet know what our plans may be.' She could not stop herself from blushing. 'Is the duke at breakfast?'

'His Grace has already eaten.' Elinor felt a stab of disappointment, but schooled her features. 'Mr Jarvis saw him riding out a while back,' the maid offered.

It was early to be riding, but perhaps her full-blooded husband felt the need of yet more vigorous exercise. The thought caused her to smile reminiscently. She swung her legs out of the bed. 'You may go, Alice. *I* will choose my gown and dress myself.'

The maid looked a trifle shocked, but Elinor ignored her. She wanted to spend time alone, time to prepare herself for the day ahead and for the husband she adored. She wondered where he might have gone. He had not mentioned riding out so early and for so long. He must be exploring the countryside, she decided, enjoying the wonderful September sun and ready to recount his adventures once he returned. It was odd, though, that he had not woken her with a goodbye kiss. Perhaps he had and she had been sleeping too soundly to remember. No, she would have known if she had been kissed. Every moment they had been together was etched deep in her memory.

She recalled the hot caresses of midnight and felt her limbs weaken. All this time later they had the power to transform her into an ardent lover again. Where was he? She wanted him. Now! She was no better than a hussy, she thought, a hussy in desperate need of self-control. This was not Elinor. But it was; it was the true Elinor set free. This was the real woman, not the grey mouse in her grey mouse dress, or the unwilling servant forced into obedience. She thought about her mother, who had been overwhelmed by desire for another Claremont. Is this how Grainne had felt? Is this why she had thrown caution to the winds, jettisoned her escape from Ireland to fall into worse trouble? For the first time since discovering her past, Elinor understood the wild beat to which her mother had danced.

Chapter Twenty-Two

Her hand was on the door, ready to descend to the breakfast room, when a knock sounded and Gabriel stood on the threshold. She smiled eagerly, but he remained where he stood. Was Summers hovering in the passage, she wondered, else why did he not take her in his arms and kiss her back to bed?

'Roland Frant is below,' he said crisply. 'He wishes to speak with you.'

She looked nonplussed. 'Roland here? What is so important that Roland has come calling today of all days?'

'I have no idea – he is stupidly mysterious. But I wish to be rid of him as soon as possible, so dismiss him when you can.'

She followed the duke down the turret stairs, her heartbeat loud in her ears. She had a premonition this visit meant trouble. Roland was waiting for them in the library, warming his hands by the small fire. He looked up as they entered the room and his smile was benign.

'You should stay, Gabriel, my tidings will prove as interesting to you as to your wife.' His voice slid sleekly over the word "wife".

All three of them remained standing, their stiff figures making a circle as though they were about to embark on a country dance.

'As you know I have been to Norfolk,' Roland began portentously. 'It was there I learned this most interesting news. The friend my mother is visiting in Norwich once lived on the Amersham estate. It was many years ago, you understand, but I learned from her information I believe to be crucial for Elinor.'

'Whatever can it be?'

'Yes, whatever can it be?' was Gabriel's sardonic echo.

Roland ignored him and turned to Elinor. 'I know it has been most important for you to discover your true identity, Cousin Elinor – although after what I have to reveal, perhaps no longer cousin?'

'What is your meaning?' Gabriel interrupted angrily. 'For once in your life be a man and spit it out.'

His cousin looked affronted. 'I have come with good news. Elinor must be anxious to know her true family.'

'You know something we have not yet discovered, Roland?' Her barely suppressed fervour was all he could desire.

'My mother's friend, a Mrs Warrinder, is now house-bound and has little contact with the outside world, but when Lady Frant spoke to her of your marriage she was most interested. You see, she knew of your mother! She recognised her name straightaway. She was a young woman who lived locally, she said. The painter – she painted miniatures.'

'Yes, yes,' Gabriel said impatiently while Elinor lowered

her eyes in disappointment.

'You are already aware of this, I know, but what Mrs Warrinder went on to say is entirely new. She said the young lady, Elinor's mother, painted while her husband tended the woods at Amersham. They were a handsome couple, she remembered, but they moved away quite suddenly and she had no notion what happened to them afterwards.'

Elinor's lips parted in surprise and her eyes widened. She was staring at Roland's face as though hypnotised.

'Explain yourself, Frant.' Gabriel's tone had lost its irony and was tinged with threat.

'It would seem Elinor's father was a forester,' Roland announced with a flourish. And then added unnecessarily, 'He was not, after all, Uncle Charles.'

There was complete silence in the room. Roland Frant looked from one to the other of his listeners. 'It is surely desirable that Elinor knows her true father. In my view Charles was always a doubtful contender.'

'This is a bag of moonshine.' Gabriel sprung into speech. 'We have evidence...' The uncertainty of that evidence hit him, but then mustering his remaining armoury, he continued, '...and your informant is an old woman, you said so yourself. Housebound. Her mind no doubt wanders. She will have confused people from her past.'

Roland smiled serenely. 'I think there is little doubt that what she says is true, cousin. And if you think carefully, it makes much more sense than Uncle Charles ever did. And after all, it changes nothing, does it? You are happily married and whether Elinor is the daughter of Charles Claremont or a humble woodsman is immaterial. Now if you will excuse me...'

And with that Roland bowed his way out of the Amersham drawing room, a satisfied smirk on his face.

They were left looking at each other, bewildered by the bombshell he had dropped. Gabriel was the first to recover. 'This must be a shock for you and you will need time to accustom yourself. But whoever your father may be, your name is or was, Milford. Your identity is not wholly lost.'

Elinor said nothing, too dumbstruck to speak. Her husband, though, seemed impelled to fill the silence. 'Think for a minute and you'll see it is good news. You escape the ignominy of having Charles Claremont as your relative!' He was trying to make light of Roland's devastating visit. 'You must not refine too much on what has happened. My wretched cousin was at least right when he said that whatever your parentage, it changes nothing.'

'I suppose not,' she said in a small voice and began to move towards him, seeking reassurance.

'I will leave you to think it over.' He strode briskly towards the door. 'Joffey has papers awaiting my signature, but we will talk more at supper.' And he was out of the room before she caught her next breath.

Was it true that it changed nothing? Gabriel insisted it was so and had tried to mollify her with surface cheer. But that was a sham. It *had* changed things. He had fled from her without a word of affection, leaving her alone and troubled, and after a night in which she had thought herself truly loved. It could only be because she was no longer the woman he had taken her for, no longer the relation he'd imagined. He had married in part to redeem his uncle's conduct so how could Roland's news not have an effect? Yesterday they had been happy in each other's company and planning their future together. Today Gabriel could not wait to leave her. Last night he had uttered words of love, but this morning those words had been rendered null, based as they were on a false premise.

She slumped down into an armchair and gazed blindly through the window at the blazing red and gold of the autumn trees. She must stop this speculation, she scolded herself, she was allowing her fears to run away with her. Gabriel disliked his cousin intensely and had been irritated to have his ride interrupted and his morning's business postponed. That was enough to explain his hasty departure.

But was it? Her mind was off again. Would he not feel he'd been trapped into marriage by her claim that Charles Claremont was her father? Surely he was bound to. He would see her differently now, not the courageous girl braving the grandeur of Amersham to find the truth, but a deliberate imposter, a deliberate deceiver. The daughter of a forester who had plotted to marry above her station. And her passionate love for him, would that not be viewed askance, too? If she could deceive in one way, she could deceive in others. He would be shocked by the desire she had shown, by her willingness to give herself to him, and he would suspect that she was not a pure woman. As a gentleman he would not reproach, but she would be silently accused and silently judged. A cavernous breach would open between them, a breach so wide that not even a marriage of convenience could bridge it.

꙳

Gabriel sat motionless, untouched papers scattered across his desk. He had been left battered by the morning's revelations: that he was capable of loving and that Elinor was capable of deception. But he could not think of her so. He remembered their search of the cellar and her glowing face when she had found the letter from the enquiry agent, her bubbling joy as he'd deciphered the singed journal entry. She had truly believed she was the daughter of Charles, 4th Duke of Amersham. No, it was rather that he had deceived himself. He had jumped to conclusions because he had wanted them to be true. By accepting her as a Claremont, he had given himself a reason to keep her close, even while he knew in his heart it was the most dangerous thing he could do.

In truth he cared nothing for Elinor's birth, whether she was a Claremont or daughter of a humble forester. Roland Frant's informant could be wrong or perhaps not even exist; the man was a scoundrel who meant nothing but wickedness. His cousin's intervention was trifling. What truly mattered were the feelings that threatened to overwhelm him. Roland's disclosure had simply laid bare the truth. He had chosen to believe Elinor's history because he had loved her from the very beginning. And he had married for the same reason, not to recompense a spurned orphan or to provide an heir for Amersham. She had woven her magic from the time she'd arrived and unleashed the most powerful emotions in him. He was confused and baffled and terrified by this new vulnerability. From this time on, he decided, they must lead separate lives.

⌒

Dinner that night was eaten in near silence. The presence of servants prevented any private discussion and Elinor had to be content with a fitful conversation on estate matters. And whenever Gabriel spoke, it was to sound dispassionate. She could not help comparing this evening with last night's wedding supper when she had sat nervously anticipating the hours ahead but relishing his admiration.

The last dishes were being removed when he said, 'I have some work to finish this evening, Elinor. I hope you will excuse me.'

Her heart was crushed small. There was to be no intimate talk between them. She flushed at the thought that once again he could not wait to leave her. He walked around the table and offered her his arm, the gesture punctilious rather than loving. Together they walked into the great flagged hall and she felt the weight of his ancestors bearing down on her. She could almost hear their cries of *imposter*. This surely was what Gabriel was thinking.

He escorted her to the foot of the huge oak staircase before saying, 'You will wish to retire. It has been a difficult day for you.'

For a moment his hand was on hers and she felt a pleasurable shiver. Deep blue eyes gazed intently into misty green and she felt the pull at her soul and the melt of her body. They stood for what seemed an age, his hand moving slowly up her inner arm, stroking its soft white skin until his fingers were reaching out to cup the swell of her bosom. She held her breath, willing him to kiss her, indifferent to the possibility of being seen. She wanted this; she wanted him so very badly.

But then it was as though he jerked himself awake. His hand was swiftly withdrawn and with a brief bow he was making his way to his study at the far end of the hall, leaving her to mount the stairs to her room alone. Alice was waiting as she had been twenty-four hours ago. The beautiful nightgown trimmed with guipure lace was laid out on the bed as it had been the night before. But with what difference.

When the maid had gone, she lay quietly, her candle still burning, her mind still busy. She had gone terribly awry, she saw that now, for she had mistaken last night's passion for love. This was indeed a marriage of convenience and love had no place in it. Gabriel had taken her with pleasure, but nothing more. And now that he doubted the very basis on which he'd married, he did not even wish for pleasure. In her search for her mother's history, she had persuaded him Charles Claremont had deceived his family. Now the tables were turned. She was the deceiver, not his uncle. She had to talk to him, convince him that she had not set out to dupe, that she had been as misled by what they had found as he. Surely he would believe her since he must want the marriage to succeed, if only to ensure an heir. If he came to her tonight they could talk and make good their misunderstanding. She would stay awake and wait for him. He would come, she told herself, the door would open and he would be there and she would abandon herself to the night and to him. He would come. But he did not.

Chapter Twenty-Three

September flowed into October, the days growing shorter but to Elinor seeming endless. She tried to occupy herself with work in the library or with walking in the gardens, but her enthusiasm had withered and the landscape had long ago lost its golden sheen. Every evening she sat opposite her husband and picked at whatever indulgence Cook had prepared while Gabriel talked of this and that, but nothing of importance to either of them. If she dared to mention Roland's information, the duke would brush it irritably to one side. 'Really, Elinor, it matters not. You must not allow yourself to mind so dearly.' Then he would lead her to the staircase, his hand barely touching her arm, bow a courteous goodnight and walk away. The spark of hope that still fluttered within her was nightly extinguished.

Alice was careful to maintain a stream of idle chatter while she undressed her mistress. Elinor could see the girl was perplexed by the duke's conduct and concerned that her mistress was growing tireder by the day. She slept little. Every night the bed grew larger, a fragile raft amid a raging sea. She was drowning and when she reached out for a comforting hand there was none. She was completely alone. She would toss and turn while the Great Hall clock struck one hour after another, until finally she fell exhausted into a troubled sleep.

Her lethargy did not pass unnoticed by Gabriel, but he steeled himself against enquiry since that could only break down the barriers he had been busy building. He was as determined as ever to recast their marriage as one of measured affection. He must treat her as a friend, a useful helpmeet, but nothing more. Only then would he be able to share her bed without the tumultuous emotions that terrified him. If he were ever foolish enough to allow himself to love, there could be only one outcome – lacerating pain – and he could bear no more. If he lost her, he would not want to continue living. And he would surely lose her. That was the pattern of his life.

During the day he applied himself to the management of the estate with an energy that made his bailiff stare, but Elinor was never far from his mind. And nightly his resolution was tempted. Somehow he found the strength to make the long walk from staircase to study, but he didn't know how long he could continue to live in this way. It was Joffey's remark that set him wondering – that when His Grace had the time, perhaps he would give consideration to his London home since the renovations at Claremont House had made little headway. If he went to London, Gabriel thought, and took Elinor with him, surely things would be easier. It was living at Amersham in close society with each other and without other distraction that was so difficult. The capital would provide all kinds of diversion and for Elinor, who had never stayed in the greatest city in the world, it could only mean pleasure. She would regain her spirits and he would regain peace of mind.

Once decided upon, he went immediately to propose the visit. It was just past noon and she was likely to have retired to her room before taking her usual light luncheon. He sprang up the oak staircase, a renewed energy coursing through him. He had found the solution to their problem and he could not imagine why he had not thought of it before. He could ask her for help in overseeing the renovations. The kitchen was in need of remodelling and every bedroom required new furnishings. What woman did not enjoy taking charge of such refurbishment? He was happy to foot any size bill if it made their life easier.

He knocked quietly at her door but there was no answer. He wondered if he had missed her on the stairs since he had already checked the library on his way up. He knocked again, and when there was still no response opened the door meaning to make sure of her absence.

A loud splash greeted him. Elinor was scrambling out of the bath and reaching for a towel to cover her nakedness. 'I'm sorry you find me so,' she flustered, 'but I have been working in the library, its furthest corner, and have become unbelievably dirty.'

He stood, overwhelmed by her loveliness, unable to speak or to move. Then he began to walk towards her, slowly, mechanically, as though stripped of all will, and plucked the towel from its wooden rail. She reached out, her face pink with embarrassment. He did not hand her the length of linen, but instead wrapped it around her shoulders and pulled her tightly towards him. They stood enwrapped, body to body, and he grew hard with longing. As his hands slid down her soft shoulders, the towel slipped from his grasp. He knelt to retrieve it, brushing her bare stomach with his mouth as he bent. He felt her shudder beneath his touch. Then his hands were on her breasts rearranging the towel, but in truth caressing her, stroke by stroke. She had undone his shirt and he scattered small kisses on her hair, her cheeks, her breasts. He was moving against her, clutching her slender form to his nakedness, at once dreamlike and urgent.

The door opened. 'Beg pardon, ma'am, Your Grace.' A scarlet-faced Alice backed hastily out of the room and the moment was broken.

He longed to consign Alice to the devil, but knew she was his saviour. In a moment he was dressed and Elinor, blushing with confusion, had covered herself with the scanty piece of cloth.

'Forgive me. I had no intention of embarrassing you.'

The words were jerked out of him. He felt as though his heart had stopped and his breath come to a juddering halt. He wanted to love her. He wanted her more than anything he had ever wanted in the world. But he must not. He must walk away. He must remove himself to a safe distance.

'I came to tell you I must go away for a short while.' His earlier plan was shot to pieces. He could no longer take his wife to London since he knew that he could not trust himself even among the distractions of the city.

She looked blank, hearing the words but not under-standing them, and he continued, 'I will be travelling to

London tomorrow.'

'This is a sudden decision,' she managed.

'I am sorry for it. Joffey has asked I make an urgent visit to Claremont House.' He excused himself the small lie.

She gave a nervous little cough. 'I would be happy to accompany you, even at this short notice. It would not take long for Alice to lay up a few items of clothing for my immediate use and then follow on with the rest of our luggage.'

His tanned face paled a little and he avoided meeting her eyes. 'That is most kind in you, my dear, but I think it best I go alone. Claremont House is undergoing refurbishment and I am not sure what I shall find.'

'A little dirt and untidiness would not signify.'

'It is likely to be a great deal more than a little.' He heard his voice grow hard and inflexible. 'You may be assured that as soon as I feel the house is in a fit state, I will return or send a message for you to join me.'

'But there is something I...'

He had to get out of the room. Her beautiful body was too close, too inviting, undoing him with its promise. He put on his most severe voice. 'Elinor, you must learn that duchess though you may be, my wishes are paramount. Now I must go, I have arrangements to make.'

And he turned on his heel before she could say or do anything to keep him there.

⌒

She slept little that night and awoke at dawn to the sound of a carriage travelling swiftly down the gravel drive. Gabriel had gone. Only a few hours previously they had come close to destroying the barriers that separated them, but in the click of a finger the moment had withered. He had looked away, turned away, and instead of loving her had announced his departure to London. He could not forget or forgive. Her deception was like a living wall between them, growing by the day, monumental and unscaleable.

Again and again she had tried to talk to him and again and again failed. Failed dismally. He would not allow her to speak. It was as though he could not bear to face his worst fears: that she was a liar, a fortune hunter, perhaps even an impure woman. She had only to mention Roland's name and Gabriel would change the subject, tell her that whatever Frant had said was unimportant. But it *was* important, desperately important, else why had he torn himself away at such a moment?

It was more urgent than ever that she talk to him, yet he had given her no chance. Days ago she had begun to feel unwell, but had hoped the nausea would pass. This morning it could not be ignored. She had bounded out of bed and managed to get to the wash bowl before she began to retch violently. Alice had come in as the spasms subsided and found her mistress clinging to the dresser, too weak to move. With her maid's help, she had regained the safety of the bed and her colour had slowly returned.

'You're not at all well, Your Grace,' the maid had tutted, 'You'll feel a deal better after a day in bed.'

But she had not stayed in bed since she had no wish for the household to guess at her indisposition. After a cup of apple cider and honey, she had repaired to the library to resume her work, but all the time her mind was elsewhere.

Suspicions she had hardly dare voice were now almost certain and she faced the dilemma of how best to break the news to a man who had been her husband for only one night. Yesterday when he had held her close to him for the first time in weeks, it had seemed a God-given opportunity. Then it had disappeared like mist in the sun and all she had been able to do was implore him to stay and hear the words she found so difficult to speak. But before she could even begin, he had turned on his heel.

And now he was gone and the day stretched wearily before her. In an echo of her mood the rain fell constantly, lashing itself against the old stone walls and turning the Hall cold and dank. She tried to remember the summer that had passed: the hours in the dairy when the sun had warmed her tired limbs, the stolen visit to the mystical circle where Gabriel had first spoken to her as a friend and the day at the fair when he had bought her flowers for her dress and she had dared to wear them. How long ago those days seemed. Even the bright September morning when she had walked to the chapel, dressed in silver gauze, seemed an aeon away. She wondered what the fortune teller would say now. She had become the duchess her mother should have been, she had fulfilled the wish of her mother's spirit, but how could Grainne ever rest knowing her daughter's unhappiness?

The rain finally petered out in late afternoon and the Great Hall clock was striking four when she donned raincoat and stout shoes. Thinking always of Gabriel, she retraced the steps she had taken with him while she was still a dairymaid, through the wood to the magical clearing and then to the meadows beyond. In turn they gave way to a slope of the Downs which rose steeply from their furthermost edge. She had never before ventured so far, but the stiff climb temporarily distracted her from her troubles and she arrived at the hill's summit breathless but a little more cheerful.

She stretched the aching muscles of her legs and took in the view. From this vantage point it was magnificent even in the fading light. Pasture land spread between the Downs like an immense green tablecloth, and in the middle of this rich valley Amersham Hall rose proud and defiant, its crenellated towers reaching for the sky. If she shaded her eyes, she could just make out the gravel circle in front of the house. A carriage stood at the front entrance, a carriage with decoration on its side panel. It had to be a crest of arms.

The duke had come home! He must have thought better of his visit to London and at some point turned his horses. She should be there to greet him, not on this distant hill trying to walk away unhappiness. She flew down the steep slope, sped across the tranquil enclosure and raced through the woods. Once she reached the drive, she walked as fast as dignity would allow, arriving at the Hall with flushed face and bedraggled hair.

But as soon as she entered the house, it was evident the duke's carriage had returned without its owner. She looked back through the open door and saw the horses being led away to the stables. Parsons was making his way to the servants' hall and tipped his hat to her. The coachman, it seemed, bore no message, no intimation of when the duke might return or when she herself might go to London. A veil of unshed tears clouded her vision and she walked blindly past the servants to the refuge of her room.

That evening she sat alone at her sitting room window, staring through the darkness and thinking, thinking, until she felt her head would fly apart. When Thomas came to pull the curtains she asked him to leave them, when Jarvis came to tell her Cook had prepared a particularly appetising dinner, she told him she required no meal that evening and when Alice came to help her to bed, she refused the maid's offer and said she would prefer to stay just where she was.

She stayed there all night. In the small hours the fire flickered out, leaving only a residue of smouldering embers, and she shivered in the cold. But wrapped in the cashmere shawl Alice had so thoughtfully left, she remained where she was. In her heart, she knew the marriage was over. It had never really started. Their one night of passion had offered false hopes that perished in the morning light. Gabriel had never promised love and she had married in full knowledge of the contract she was entering, but in a foolish fantasy she had dreamed that he might one day love her as much as she loved him. It had been just that – a fantasy. Like Grainne she had fallen for a man unable to return her deepest feelings. But the situation was worse than that, far worse. She had fallen for a man who did not even like her, a man who could not bear to be in her company. Even if he were to return tomorrow, it would make no difference. Gabriel would never confess his doubts, never confide his lack of trust, never give her the chance to make things right. He would brush her aside and simply go on as before.

She could not continue to live in this way, especially not now. Once it was known she was with child, she would be tied to Amersham and tied to a forlorn marriage. Their baby would grow to maturity in an unhappy house, as unhappy as any Gabriel himself had known. She could not contemplate such an outcome. So what was the remedy? It was drastic, but it had to be. The only solution was to disappear so completely that Gabriel would be unable to trace her. More likely he would not try since he would be relieved to have the façade of their marriage shattered. He would be free to file for annulment and marry a woman of his own class, who would give him the heir he needed.

And what of her? She was strong, she told herself, and despite the heartbreak she would walk from Amersham with her head held high. She would don her grey dress and pack her portmanteau for the last time. She would do as her mother had done all those years ago and cast herself upon the world.

Chapter Twenty-Four

Her step was lighter than it had been for days when the next morning she took a last walk in the Hall gardens. She might be nursing a raw heart, but the decision was made and for that she was thankful. As she turned back to the house, she was surprised to see Roland Frant making his way towards her across the damp grass.

'Good day,' he hailed her cheerfully. 'For once the sun is shining and you are right to take advantage. But this grass has my feet soaking.'

'Mine too. But I cannot be for ever indoors. Were you on your way to see me?' He has come to discover why Gabriel is absent, she thought.

'I was about to leave you these journals,' and he indicated the parcel he carried. 'Light reading only, but a welcome change, I hope, from the Amersham library.'

She was uncertain as to whether Gabriel's cousin was friend or enemy, but today he seemed well-disposed and she was grateful for this small attention. 'How kind of you to think of me. Won't you come into the house? I'm sure we can depend on Jarvis for a tray of tea.'

'That would be most pleasant,' he said with hardly a

pause. 'Thank you, Elinor.'

She must act as normally as possible since it would not do to arouse suspicion – he had accepted her invitation a little too eagerly. Minutes later they were in the drawing room and he had settled himself into one of the large chesterfields.

Once Jarvis had delivered the tea tray, the conversation hovered safely around mundane topics until he said, 'My mother is thinking of having a conservatory erected adjoining the south wall of the Dower House. She recently saw an illustration of the Chelsea Physic Garden and was much taken by it.'

'I imagine it would make a very pleasant room in winter as well as summer,' Elinor replied, picking her words with care. She was wary of where the subject might lead.

'It may seem a little grand for such a modest dwelling – I did have doubts at first – but I think now it will look very well. We cannot be wholly indifferent to improvements,' he offered slyly, 'especially with Claremont House receiving so much attention of late. Have you heard how the renovations are progressing?'

He had reached what he came for, she thought, and she answered him shortly. 'I have no news as yet.'

Her guest appeared undeterred. 'The work has been going on for a long time, I believe. Gabriel must have decided upon some quite elaborate changes, particularly as he has found it necessary to supervise them personally.'

'The duke wishes our London home to be perfect for me.'

'That is understandable and I imagine you cannot wait

to see what has been done.'

He seemed determined to pin her down and she went fearlessly into the fray. 'Gabriel will send a message as soon as he feels it right for me to travel. Until then, I am happy to wait.'

'You will need to leave Amersham before the roads are mired in mud. Come November, coach travel becomes a lottery in these outlying country districts. Only horseback is certain and I do not think the duke would wish his bride to ride all the way to London!'

'I am sure he has considered every difficulty.'

'I hope so, but if you will forgive me for saying, he seems to have given one consideration little thought – that of leaving you here alone.'

'It was necessary for him to travel ahead and I am quite content,' she countered falsely.

He looked at her in earnest. 'I hope you know that you may count on my assistance at any time.' A flush suffused her face and her figure stiffened, but he seemed not to notice and carried on talking. 'Forgive me, but I wish only to offer whatever aid I may.'

'I appreciate your concern, Roland, but I require no help.'

'I am pleased to hear it.'

By now she was scarlet with embarrassment and longed for him to go. She sipped her tea and a wave of nausea surged through her. She knew he was watching her closely and attempted a weak smile. It would not do to broadcast her indisposition. He would certainly tell Lady Frant and she feared what his mother would make of it – a possible heir was the last thing Celia would want. But perhaps if she knew the truth, that redoubtable woman would help her on her way.

A thought burned through her mind. She would help her on her way...not Celia though, but Roland. He could be just what she needed and while he talked on, her brain was working feverishly.

'Will you be visiting Hurstwood shortly?' He looked startled, his flow of conversation brought to a sharp close.

'I have no definite plans. Why do you ask?'

'A few days ago I received a letter from Bath, from some old friends,' she lied fluently. 'I had written telling them of my marriage. In their reply they mention they have an elderly relative living in this district. Living near to Hurstwood, in fact. They believe her to have fallen sick and have asked me to visit, if at all possible. I wish very much to oblige them in this.'

'That is most commendable, but I am unsure how I can be of assistance.'

'You have a carriage, Roland, and you have a house close to where I wish to travel. I wondered if you might soon be going there.' She smiled encouragingly at him.

'I would be delighted to escort you, my dear, but does not Amersham boast a coach and coachman? I think we should allow Parsons to do his job, don't you?'

It was an obvious point and caused her to think rapidly. 'Parsons must stay here. He has been commanded by Gabriel to await his master's instructions which could come at any time or any day.' It was horribly weak but it would have to suffice.

Roland was looking wary, but said smoothly enough, 'If that is so, I am more than happy to drive you.'

'You are most kind. Shall we say this afternoon? I can be ready shortly after midday.'

The startled expression was back and she hurried to douse any suspicions he might have. 'My friends' aunt is very frail and could leave the world at any moment. I would not like to think I arrived too late.'

Roland squared his shoulders. 'Naturally you would not. You may be sure I will return with the carriage before two hours have passed.'

'That is most kind,' she said again, as warmly as she could manage, and rose from her chair. She hoped he would take the hint and leave since nausea was again threatening and she needed to be alone. She had got what she wanted – a departure from Amersham that would be unexceptional. Not an eyebrow would be raised at the sight of her driving through the gates with Roland at her side.

❦

She was packed within the hour, but remained out of sight in her sitting room. It was fortunate Alice had been granted leave that day to visit her mother in the next village and by the time she returned, Elinor hoped to be miles from Amersham. But the afternoon wore on and Roland Frant did not appear. She became increasingly tense, hovering anxiously by the window, listening intently for the sound of carriage wheels. Was he about to let her down? By the time the clock struck four, she had taken off her bonnet and consigned her wonderful plan to the flames. But then a jingle of distant harness. Flying back to the window, she saw at last Roland's gig making its way to the front entrance. She bounded down the stairs, portmanteau in hand, and arrived breathless at the steps of the carriage almost before it had come to a halt.

Roland's eyes took in the drab grey of her dress and the large bag she carried. His forehead puckered.

'A few herbal remedies for the invalid,' she said smoothly. 'Mrs Lucas's own recipes. I'm hoping they may help a little.' He settled the portmanteau between them and indicated her gown. 'And are you dressed for nursing?'

'The gown will be more useful than silks and satins, I'm sure, but my real wish is not to intimidate the old lady by appearing too splendidly dressed.'

There was a pause while he digested this and she took advantage of his silence to deflect his questioning. 'I had thought you would be with me earlier, Roland.'

'I must apologise for keeping you waiting, but Sultan threw a shoe and the smith was a long time coming.'

'I am most grateful you arrived at all.' It would be wise to appease him, she thought. 'But do let us make haste. It will be dusk in a few hours and though I have my friends' directions, I am not entirely sure where the cottage lies.'

He nodded agreement and once out of the gates whipped his horse to a spirited pace. The miles disappeared rapidly beneath the carriage wheels, leaving Elinor little time to grieve for what she was leaving behind but reminding her instead how urgent was her present plight. She must search for lodgings in the near dark and in a countryside she did not know. They had been travelling for well over an hour when she saw they were approaching a crossroads, one artery of which was not much more than a lane. She could see a chimney smoking at some distance and made a rapid decision.

'This is it, Roland. Please pull up.'

'Where is it?' He was looking bewildered and she could hardly blame him. They had come to a halt in the middle of nowhere.

'The crossroads,' she extemporized. 'The directions mentioned the crossroads.' Thank goodness they had passed no others on the journey. 'And a cottage sitting a short way along one of its lanes. There it is, you see,' and she pointed to the chimney smoking in the distance.

Her companion swivelled his head and peered down the lane. 'You think this is the place?'

'I am sure of it.' She gathered up her bag. 'Thank you so much for your assistance. You have been kindness itself.'

'You are surely not getting down here? I will drive you to the house.'

'There is no need. I can easily walk the short distance and you must be getting back to Amersham or it will be pitch black before you arrive and that will make for a dangerous journey.'

He put out his arm to restrain her. 'There is a full moon tonight and I can return at leisure. But something feels wrong here – tell me.'

She did not reply and when he spoke again, his voice was incredulous. 'Are you running away?'

She felt her shoulders collapse, as though she were a toy devoid of its stuffing.

'You cannot be running away from Amersham!'

'I have to get away – for a while,' she murmured.

'So there is no aunt, no invalid?'

'I am most sorry for the deception, Roland. But you need have no further involvement. Allow me to get down from the carriage and then forget that you ever saw me today.'

'But where will you go?'

'I will seek a lodging, perhaps in that very cottage.' She tried a brave smile that did not quite come off. 'There is always someone willing to rent a room.'

'At this time of night?'

'I admit I would have wished to have searched in daylight, but it is of no matter.'

'You cannot wander around in the countryside in the dark,' he protested. 'You are the Duchess of Amersham!'

'No longer. My life at Amersham is finished.'

He looked astounded, but there was a suspicion of a simper at the corners of his mouth. 'Then allow me to drive you to Hurstwood. It is a mere thirty minutes away and you will have a comfortable bed for the night.'

Her expression must have conveyed her alarm at the prospect as he said in his most soothing voice, 'I will stay only to give instructions to my housekeeper, but you may remain at the house as long as you wish. I will not be returning for some days.'

'It will be for tonight alone,' she promised. 'I will be gone first thing in the morning. I cannot say where, but that is all to the good. If you have no knowledge, you cannot be held responsible for my disappearance.'

His lips curved into an outright smile. 'I do not approve

your actions, Elinor, but as you appear determined, I can only wish you well. For now I had better drive you to Hurstwood.'

~

'I cannot see why you should offer Hurstwood to that interloper,' Lady Frant protested while her son irritably divested himself of driving gloves. He had been avid to recount the day's happenings, but his mother was proving a disappointing audience.

'If Gabriel has deliberately stranded her at Amersham, it is for good reason,' Celia went on, 'and if he has not and returns shortly, you would have been well advised to have kept your distance.'

Roland looked across the table at his mother. 'I *have* kept my distance,' he said impatiently. 'Nobody saw us today and she intends to leave Hurstwood on the morrow.'

'I do not like it. If she should continue to stay at your house, we will be implicated in her flight.'

'She will not stay, I am sure. Elinor is a resourceful young woman and determined to leave the county. I thought, Mama, that at one time you were equally determined she should.'

'One time? You know very well that is still the case.'

'I thought I did, but you seem lately to have given up on the project – it has been left entirely to me. It was my initiative to relate the tale of Elinor's parentage.'

'And what was the point of that? It has made not a jot of difference.'

'On the contrary, I believe it has made all the difference. Else why has she taken such a drastic step in leaving

Amersham?'

'Only to be driven to Hurstwood,' his mother muttered.

'But don't you see that by leaving the Hall the duchess is saying the marriage is over. Gabriel will be furious and wash his hands of her completely.'

'Do not give her that title. The very thought makes me shudder. And how can you know he will react so?'

'He will consider it his prerogative to determine whether or not the marriage fails and will be very angry she has taken the matter into her own hands.'

His mother continued to look sceptical while he rose from his chair and strode around the room, his hands deep in his pockets, his brow furrowed in thought.

'I have my suspicions, Mama, and if they are true, it is imperative Elinor Milford leave Amersham as soon as possible.'

For the first time Celia Frant looked at him with interest.

'I believe her to be with child.'

His announcement had all the effect he could wish. His mother gasped aloud. 'How can you be sure?'

'Naturally I cannot be entirely sure, but she is pale and wan and she is not eating. I thought she would be sick when I took tea with her.'

'If she is indeed carrying Gabriel's child that would be a blow from which we could not recover. But if she were to disappear, to vanish from his world before he got wind of the fact...'

'Perhaps you will concede now that I have acted prudently.'

His mother nodded. 'It would seem so. But let us consider for a moment the difficulties that may yet wreck your plan.' She pursed her lips and began to tap her hand on the table, each tap a harbinger of misfortune. 'You say she is determined to leave Hurstwood tomorrow. But what if she doesn't? The house is a comfortable refuge – what if she is tempted to stay?'

'Then I will go to her with a false tale that Gabriel knows of the baby, that he is very angry and accuses her of stealing the heir to Amersham. I shall paint as black a picture as possible to the – to Elinor – then suggest she leave at once to avoid the duke finding her and punishing her for her disloyalty.'

His mother looked at him in grudging admiration. 'I would not have thought you could be so ruthless, Roland, and after seeming to befriend the girl.'

'It is for the good of Amersham,' he said solemnly. 'And I do not believe Elinor will suffer. I imagine the duke has provided financially.'

His mother was still thinking. 'Is it possible Gabriel already knows of the baby?'

'I doubt it. I cannot think he would have left her alone to travel to London.'

'No, you are right. But that does not mean he will not find out and insist his wife return to Amersham for her confinement. It is his legal right. He might allow her to disappear after the event, but he will then be in possession of an heir.'

'It could be a daughter,' he reminded her. 'But in any case, he will not find out. Who is to tell him? You? Me? She is not so far gone that the servants will have noticed. And

I am certain that within the next few days she will leave Sussex, and when she does she will leave with her secret intact.'

'And once our little upstart has disappeared, there will be no one left to keep Gabriel in check,' Celia mused. 'He has been noticeably abstemious since the night I brought her to the Dower House and, according to the bailiff, has taken the running of the estate into his own hands. She has had a beneficial influence and who knows, he might actually have a *tendre* for her and her defection could hit him hard. Without her, he will no doubt return to his old ways.'

Roland nodded enthusiastically and his mother warmed to her theme. 'People will say he has driven his bride away. He will forfeit the goodwill of his neighbours and lose any incentive to regularise his life. That can only hasten his degeneration.'

'Exactly.' Roland breathed an almost ecstatic sigh. 'Have I not been clever, Mama?' He could have been a small child awaiting his reward in bonbons.

'You have, my dear,' Celia finally conceded. 'I am already looking forward to the day when I see you rightly installed as the Duke of Amersham.'

Chapter Twenty-Five

Gabriel had been in London for less than an hour before he knew he had made a terrible mistake. Had he really thought that in journeying sixty miles he could escape his feelings? How very stupid! He had thought to save himself from pain, but coming to London had not signified salvation. Elinor had been with him every step of the journey and was with him still in every breath he took. She had been with him from the moment he had first seen her mounting the steps of the dairy, carefully managing her laden tray. He had been intrigued, fascinated, by this slender, too tall girl with a too wide mouth, just made to be kissed. But something more had set her apart from any woman he had met, something indefinable. And months on, he knew what that was – he had fallen in love. Incredibly, amazingly, he had fallen headlong in love even as he had lounged casually against the creamery walls and watched her every move. During these last solitary months at Amersham he had missed her dreadfully, and now they were miles apart every minute was cutting him to ribbons.

That night he roamed the empty mansion, room by room, unable to sleep or even rest, and when next morning, unrefreshed, he staggered into his clothes, he could not bring himself to meet the architect who waited patiently below. He had Summers offer his apologies and tried instead to distract himself by driving his new phaeton. But the expedition to Hyde Park came to a swift end. Unwilling to take part in idle conversation or even greet the many acquaintances eager to speak to him, he soon turned tail and sought sanctuary at home. The evening fared no better. A convivial reunion at Limmer's Hotel arranged by a fellow comrade-in-arms ended prematurely when, unable to tolerate their trivialities a minute longer, he stood up without a word and walked out into Hanover Square, leaving his companions stunned.

He was as much stunned as they and strode back to Mount Street with a mind in turmoil. He could not continue like this, he must go back to Amersham. But how would Elinor respond to his return? She had been entitled to expect a grain of friendship at least, a scrap of company, and he had given neither. He had rejected her every advance and left her lonely. She would rightly be angry, perhaps unforgiving. He must ask her forgiveness, try to explain. But how could he explain, how could he defend his conduct without telling her how deeply he loved her? He had to tell her, that was clear, but it would not be easy. She did not share his feelings, had not a thought of love for him, he was sure, and yet he must force himself to lay his heart bare.

Claremont House was ablaze with light as he walked through the front door, but he hardly noticed its welcome. He flung hat and gloves onto the marquetry table and made for the library. A fire flickered warmly in the grate and he strode over to adjust a burning log. He stayed there, standing for minutes on end, his hands on the marble mantelpiece, outstaring the rising flames. Somehow he must find the strength to do this.

It was the sound of the door knocker that disturbed his thoughts. It was late and he wondered who could be calling at this hour. Summers, a disapproving expression on his face, ushered the visitor into the drawing room. Gabriel understood his henchman's countenance when Weatherby strode into the room, a familiar sneer on his pallid face. The duke had seen nothing of him, nor wished to, since the man had ridden out of Amersham's gates with his fellows in the long days of summer.

His visitor appeared not to notice they had become strangers and continued to smile in an ingratiating manner. 'I heard you were in town, Gabe. I must say it's good to see you. Been a bit out of touch myself lately. Weeks in Yorkshire – fearful place, don't you know – and then the old aunt didn't do the decent thing after all. Recovered sufficiently to know who I was. Left her lying in bed, still comatose but alive.'

'How unfortunate for you both,' Gabriel responded drily.

'You win some, you lose some, but I'm feeling pretty corky being back in civilization. Deserves a drink, don't you think?'

'Bring wine, Summers,' Gabriel ordered. With luck his unwelcome guest would leave shortly for a more enticing engagement since there would be gambling at the clubs into the small hours.

Weatherby took a seat opposite and stretched himself expansively. 'You've given up the brandy, I see. Can only be a good thing. Wine doesn't rot the guts so badly.'

The duke nodded absently, but had nothing to say to his erstwhile companion. Weatherby fidgeted and began to tap his foot at the uneasy silence. Finally he was driven to enquire, 'So what brings you to London this early in winter, Gabe?'

'Things,' the duke replied vaguely. He had no wish to start a conversation that would lead back to Elinor.

'Things?'

'Yes.'

His visitor shifted impatiently and tried again. 'The Regent has been spinning a tale that you got married. Surely that's a hum?'

'No.'

'No, you didn't marry or no, it's not a bag of moonshine.'

'I married.'

Weatherby whistled through his teeth. 'So it's true! You did get married. I thought it a plumper when I heard the story but...you and the dairymaid!'

Gabriel glared fiercely at him, but the man seemed unaware of his hostility and kept on talking. 'Why, Gabe? It don't make sense. You could have had the girl for the taking. Why shackle yourself – and to a servant! My God, it's unbelievable!'

'As always your mouth spews filth, Weatherby.'

'Steady on, old chap. No wish to set up your bristles, but you must admit it's a bit of a come-out. The dairymaid reigns at Amersham or so I'm told, and the duke is banished to Mount Street.'

'You are under a misapprehension.'

'Don't think so, old chap. No wonder you're so damn miserable. You shouldn't let a woman dictate to you, especially in – um – the circumstances.'

Summers came in with wine and glasses. He arranged them carefully on the small table next to his master, but as he moved towards the door Gabriel's hand stopped him.

Weatherby, believing the servant had left, began to speak again. 'Here's an idea. Why don't we get the old crowd together and make for the Hall. We could have fun, you could have fun. Everyone needs to break out some time or another, and think of the possibilities, miles out in the countryside, no one to shock. Your dairymaid is too uppity by far. She needs to be taught a lesson, and –'

'Mr Weatherby won't, after all, be requiring wine, Summers.' Gabriel's voice was a steel blade slicing the air. 'Show him to the door.'

'No need for that,' the older man spluttered. 'No offence meant. I just –'

'Out!'

Summers took the visitor firmly by the arm. 'This way, sir,' and Weatherby was led protesting from the room. Gabriel heard the front door close with a satisfying thud.

'How did I ever mix with people like that?' he asked when Summers returned. 'I must have been out of my mind.' He kicked angrily at the fender.

'In a manner of speaking, Your Grace, you were. You had much to bear.'

'But to make such scoundrels my companions!'

'They weren't suitable, Your Grace, that's for sure, but in the circumstances it was understandable.'

'You're too kind, Summers.'

'No, sir, I've an inkling of what you've been through. Don't forget Master Jonathan was my charge.' He spoke with the familiarity of a man who for years had been the brothers' friend and mentor, rescuing them from the dangers of boyhood and later, willingly sharing the hardships of war.

'You loved him too, I know. I've been damnably selfish.'

'You had a right. Life has been difficult. Being a duke isn't all that it's cracked up to be, not when there's no love around.'

The duke looked at him sharply. 'Is there something you wish to say, Summers?'

'Reckon I don't need to.'

Gabriel looked at him for a long moment, then straightened his shoulders and strode to the door. 'You're right. You don't.'

The encounter with Weatherby had crystallised the desperate longing that haunted him. His love for Elinor could not wait another minute. 'Send to the stables for a saddle horse. There's no need to pack a bag – I have all I need at Amersham.'

'We're going to Amersham, Your Grace?'

'*I* am going. You can follow later. I am going home, Summers.'

His manservant beamed. 'Yes, Your Grace.'

It was night black when Gabriel began the cross-country ride to his Sussex home, but he knew the way by heart and had no fear he would go astray. He wanted to be at the Hall as the sun rose, wanted to walk into Elinor's room and kiss her awake. He would lie beside her and enfold her in his arms. He would make his confession. He would love her in the way he had longed to, night after lonely night.

He was riding to reclaim his wife. The words echoed and re-echoed in his mind, rung through with a new and joyful energy. Once out of London he travelled swiftly, but was careful to pace his horse for the long journey ahead. The miles flew as he took to the lanes and by-ways he knew so well. How many times had he and Jonathan ridden this route? Driving a carriage to London had been too tame for them. Instead they had arrived at Claremont House hot, dirty and tired. But they had felt alive, so alive – in the way he felt right now.

He reached Steyning an hour after dawn and slowed the horse to a walk. There were five miles still to cover, but he had made excellent time despite the lingering mist, and could afford to rest the mare. Once back in open country-side, he picked up speed again, his yearning to see Elinor's lovely face paramount. Then he was at the gates, at the stables where he turned the horse over to a yawning lad, and then onto the house. He bounded up the stairs two at a time, paused for a moment at the threshold of her room, and then quietly opened the door.

The room was bathed in light for the curtains were already open. Had she risen so very early?

'Elinor,' he called softly. 'Elinor?' He walked towards

the bed. It was empty and disappointment seared him. He had imagined this meeting through every one of the long night's miles and she was not here. He looked back at the bed – but surely it had not been slept in!

He strode to the bell pull and tugged sharply. Alice appeared on the instant, a scared look on her face.

'Where is the duchess?'

'She's not here, Your Grace.'

'I can see that for myself.'

The girl looked even more frightened and Gabriel softened his tone. 'Alice, what has happened to your mistress?'

'I don't rightly know, sir.' The maid in her agitation crumpled her apron. 'I was away at my mother's yesterday and when I got back Her Grace was gone.'

'Gone? Did no one look for her?'

'It were late, Your Grace. The household were asleep when I got back. I woke Mr Jarvis and he thought my lady might have gone to London to be with you. He said we would have to wait until it was light before we could find out. I've been awake all night in case Her Grace returned.'

'But if she had gone to London, Parsons would have driven her. Has he gone too? Has anyone checked?'

'Parsons is eating breakfast downstairs,' Alice said miserably.

'And did no one see her leave?'

'No one, Your Grace. Mr Jarvis has this minute finished asking.'

Gabriel sunk down on a chair, his head in his hands. If she was not at the Hall and had not crossed his path in travelling to London, where was she? And where had she spent the night? She could be sick or in danger and he was powerless to go to her rescue. Alice stood close by, her head bowed and a small tear making its uneven way down her cheek.

'Perhaps she has not gone so far.' Gabriel sprung up, filled with a new hope. It was unlikely but possible that she was staying at the Dower House. 'Are her clothes here?'

'I didn't look, Your Grace. I'm sorry.'

'Look now.'

Alice opened the wardrobes, one after another. 'There's nothing missing, sir,' she puzzled.

'Yes, there is.' Gabriel was grimly surveying the wardrobe's contents. 'The grey dress she wore when she first came to us. Where is that?'

'It's there, in that corner... It ain't there any longer.'

'And her portmanteau?'

Alice checked the floor of the wardrobe. 'Gone too, sir.'

The duke walked to the window and looked blindly down the drive he had just traversed. Elinor had taken what belonged to her and nothing more. She had put on her old dress and packed her old bag and left behind the trappings of a duchess. There was a finality to her actions and he knew she had left for good. How could she have done that when he loved her from the bottom of his heart? But that was something she could not know. He had pushed her away day after day without explanation and she had decided to take the future into her own hands. He heard her voice in his ear – did she not believe that everyone's destiny was theirs to determine?

A quiet knock at the door and Jarvis stood on the

threshold. Gabriel leapt to his feet. 'You have news?'

'Ben has something to say, Your Grace,' and he pushed the youngest stable boy into the room. The boy hung his head and seemed unable to open his mouth.

'Go on, boy.' The butler dug him in the ribs. 'Tell His Grace what you've just told me.'

'I sawed 'er,' the boy mumbled.

'Her? The duchess?'

The boy nodded. 'Where?' Gabriel asked hungrily.

'Goin' down the drive.'

'And?'

'She were in a carridge.'

'Your Grace,' interpolated Mr Jarvis, looking severely at his junior.

'Never mind that. Whose carriage, Ben?' The butler gave the boy another sharp nudge.

'Mister Frant's.'

The duke fixed him with a penetrating stare. 'Are you absolutely sure?'

'Yessir.'

'And who was driving?'

'Mister Frant.'

Jarvis made to hurry the boy from the room saying as he did, 'Would you wish me to send to the Dower House for Mr Frant, Your Grace?'

Gabriel's brow was dark and his face contorted. 'No, Jarvis. Allow me to surprise him.'

He pushed past his retainers and was down the stairs before they could stop him.

Chapter Twenty-Six

'Where is he?'

A loud altercation brought Lady Frant, looking less than her polished best, flying down the stairs.

'What are you doing here at this hour, Gabriel? You cannot barge your way into my house in this manner. Please leave!'

'A landlord is entitled to enter his own property – and stay there if he so wishes,' her nephew retaliated. 'I've no intention of leaving.'

Celia's voice dropped to a placatory murmur. 'You are very welcome to return later, Your Grace, but I must ask you to leave now. It is far too early.'

'A tenant cannot lay down such conditions.'

Lady Frant abandoned all pleasantries and went in fighting. 'What nonsense is this? How dare you speak so to your father's sister? I am no ordinary tenant.'

'Certainly you are not. No ordinary tenant would have planned so cleverly to whisk my wife from her home without anyone knowing.'

There was a silence before Celia spoke, her voice

shamming ignorance. 'I have no notion of your meaning.'

'Have you not? Then let me inform you. Elinor is missing from Amersham. She left yesterday in a carriage driven by your son. Does that help? Do not bother to deny it. I have a stable boy who saw them with his own eyes.'

'I have no knowledge of such an event. I can only think your servant's imagination verges on the vivid.'

'We'll put it to the test, shall we?' She felt herself unceremoniously pushed aside and forced to watch helplessly as Gabriel took the stairs two at a time.

'You would not conduct yourself so arrogantly if Roland *were* here,' she called after him.

Gabriel paused mid-flight, turning to face her. 'He is here, of that I'm sure. But he will wish himself elsewhere when I have finished with him. You will both wish yourselves elsewhere – indeed, you may start packing now.'

Roland Frant appeared on the landing as the duke reached the top of the stairs. He might have been woken by the commotion below, Gabriel thought grimly, but he was still alert enough to be fully dressed.

'I must echo my mother's words, Gabriel,' his cousin began, 'and ask you to leave. I imagine this outrageous intrusion is a result of your drinking. I would advise –'

But Gabriel was not in the mood to take advice. He sprang towards Roland and grabbed him by the throat. The man's complexion mottled violently until it was almost purple and a strange whimpering noise came from deep within his chest. He struggled in vain to free himself but the duke's grip was iron, slowly squeezing the life out of him.

'Where is she, you little rat? Tell me!'

Roland's arms waved frantically in the air. The duke allowed his grasp to loosen very slightly.

'Your Grace, please I beg of you,' Roland panted.

'Keep begging and I may let you live. Where is she?'

'Hurstwood,' his cousin whimpered in a voice grating with pain.

'Hurstwood? Then you are a bigger villain than I took you for.' Gabriel's hands began to tighten around the man's throat once more.

'No,' he managed to gasp, 'she was running away and I did nothing but help her reach safety.'

Gabriel drew himself upright and looked scornfully down on the speaker. 'Nothing but put her in the greatest of danger. You are a dog.' And he cast Roland down on to the floor where his cousin lay in a sobbing heap.

He was half way down the stairs when a voice barely above a whisper croaked, 'You'll pay for this. Name your seconds.'

'I would,' the duke spat the words, 'if I thought for one moment a cur such as you would dare to meet me. I am more than happy to run you through any time of your choosing. You know where to find me.'

Roland said nothing.

'I thought not,' Gabriel threw over his shoulder and walked out.

⌒

He was almost at Hurstwood and still the mist had not cleared. The road here dwindled into little more than a track, empty at this time of the morning, since it was too early for even the carrier to be making his daily deliveries. Intent on reaching the house, Gabriel pushed the horse into a canter once more, feathered a blind bend and almost collided with a grey figure emerging spectre-like from out of the morning haze. The figure gave a startled cry and leapt aside. He pulled fiercely on the reins and was out of the saddle in a trice, his arm outstretched to help. The woman took his hand in a firm grip and clambered back up the bank and onto the road. They stood facing each other.

'Elinor!'

'You!'

It was not the most auspicious beginning. Her face was pink with vexation and her hands began agitatedly adjusting the skirts of her dress. But when she spoke her voice was strong and clear. 'I have left Amersham, Gabriel, and wish to continue my journey. I hope you will not make it difficult.'

He was grappling with the horror of her words and could only stammer, 'How could you leave without a word to me?'

'There is nothing to say.' She sounded unnaturally composed. 'You have made your decision and I must make mine.'

'I have made no decision.' His voice expressed bewilderment. 'I know I have caused you distress and I'm sorry – abjectly so. But can we not talk of this?'

'Why? We have not managed to do so before.'

And she picked up her battered portmanteau and slipped beneath his outstretched arm. She had hardly gone a step before her ankle gave way and she would have fallen but for Gabriel's strong hold.

'See what you have done.' She hastily brushed away the tears that were threatening. 'I cannot walk, thanks to your recklessness.'

He forbore to point out that their collision had been an accident, that she had been walking a narrow lane shrouded in mist. Instead he tried to plead for time.

'If you are intent on leaving, I cannot stop you, but at least let me drive you to wherever you wish. Or if you will not accept my escort, let me put my coachman at your disposal.'

She looked as though she wanted to argue, but she was in no position to travel unaided and he gave thanks for the small blessing. 'If you'll return with me to the Hall, I will order the carriage to be made ready.'

'It would seem I have little choice,' she said wearily.

He tossed her up into the saddle, handed up her luggage, and then mounted behind her. 'It won't be the first time that we have ridden bodkin,' he said as cheerfully as he could. It was not the first time, but this was going to be a vastly different ride.

⌒

Elinor sat straight in the saddle, as far forward as she could manage. She must maintain whatever small space there was between them. She had no wish to remember the last time she had shared a horse with Gabriel. Then she had lain against him, felt his body enfolding her, and wanted the ride to go on for ever. Now she was desperate for it to end. And when it ended, what could either of them say? Her unwitting deception had divided them, troubling him so badly he had abandoned her. Was it likely that two days' absence had changed his mind?

The journey to Amersham was wearisome and they were both relieved when its huge iron gates loomed out of the distance. Once on the carriage way, the mare, sensing the closeness the stables, picked up her heels in anticipation. But without warning Gabriel left the well-trodden drive and veered across the grass towards the woods that he and Elinor had walked all those months ago. She tried to turn her head to protest, but her words were carried away on the air.

He leaned forward and spoke into her ear. 'I thought to take a small detour – for an hour at most. Then we will go to the Hall and order the carriage.' She could do nothing but acquiesce.

They were in the woods now and the chill of the morning still hung in the branches above. She shivered and for a moment wished Gabriel would move closer. But she should be glad he did not; she had made the right choice in leaving and she must keep to her purpose. They travelled along the uneven path, the horse carefully stepping between tree roots and through patches of undergrowth, on and on until the sky began to brighten and the trees give way to open space. A perfect sphere of light appeared ahead. They had arrived at the clearing.

Gabriel slid from the saddle and came to the horse's head.

'Why are we here?' Her nervousness was making her pettish.

'We are here because I must tell you something before

you leave, and this feels the right place.'

The hushed circle brought back memories, unbearably happy memories, and she was stung into unwise words. 'But not for me, not for what I have to tell.'

She felt a deep yearning to speak of the baby she carried, but she knew she must keep silent. No more foolish retorts, she chided herself. If she told, she would never be able to leave. And she had to. She could not bear to live another day in this loveless marriage.

He reached up for her and put his hands around her waist to lift her from the saddle. She felt the strong, firm clasp on her body and had an insane urge to cling to him, but schooled herself to break away. He led her to where they had sat once before on that bright June morning. The felled oak was still there and a full sun rising over the clearing made the place look much as it had months ago. Only they had changed. The surrounding trees lifted their heads to the new warmth, their autumn dress of red and gold glowing in the morning rays. A bird somewhere sang out its joy and everywhere was still. She could have stayed there for ever. But peace such as this was not to be hers; she had a journey to make, she reminded herself.

They sat quietly side by side on the fallen tree and she could almost hear their two hearts beating. Then he turned to her with a strange smile, a shy smile.

'What I have to say is very simple,' he said after a long pause. 'I love you. I love you, Elinor.'

Chapter Twenty-Seven

It was an extraordinary declaration. An unbelievable declaration. 'But -' she began.

'I know what you will say and you are right. I have behaved as stupidly as any man could. But stupidity *was* to blame, not lack of love. I was afraid, afraid of the feelings you aroused in me and I walked away.'

She could hardly credit his words. 'You left because you loved me!'

'I did mention the word stupidity, didn't I?' He turned his head towards her, willing her to look at him. 'I offered you a marriage of convenience, a business arrangement, but I don't think I ever believed in it. I loved you from the first moment I saw you, but I kept pretending to myself that I felt no such thing. When we found Charles' papers and it seemed almost certain we were in some way related, I was delighted. More than delighted. I could keep you at Amersham. Not only that, I could bring you even closer by moving you into the Hall.'

'But you haven't wanted to be near me.'

'Of course I have. I have not dared to be near you. I couldn't trust myself. I've longed for you to be close, but couldn't bear it when you *were* close. Does that make any sense?'

His question floated in the still air. 'In a strange way, I suppose,' she said slowly. 'But if I bothered you so much, why did you choose to marry?'

'I told myself marriage would benefit us both. I could give you back your rightful home and at the same time provide Amersham with an heir. It all made perfect sense. Except the story I told myself wasn't true, and on our wedding night the façade I'd built collapsed into ruins.'

His fingers drummed a ragged beat against the tree's bark. There was a long pause before he spoke again and when he did, his voice was shaky with emotion. 'The truth was I loved you with all the passion I was capable of, and I wanted to go on loving you like that for ever. I couldn't pretend to myself any more.'

'But you didn't do that. You didn't go on loving me. It makes no sense after all, Gabriel.'

'It does to someone who has been hurt very badly.'

She did not respond immediately. Instead she sat and thought. Thought of his parents who had gone away while he was still a small child and never returned, of an uncle who had offered only contempt, of a much loved brother who had died on a far-away battlefield. The scars had cut deep and she understood that. But what then of her deceit?

She found herself stuttering the question that mattered so much. 'And my parentage?'

'What about it?'

'You were deceived. Charles Claremont is not my father.'

'We don't know that. I have a strong suspicion Roland's

tale is yet another mischief. I've asked my London agent to travel to Norwich and interview this Mrs Warrinder. I think we will find she knows nothing of you or your parents. But even if she does and your father turns out to be a trusty woodsman, do you think I really care?'

'I believed you did. I believed you cared a great deal.'

He looked bewildered. 'You thought I cared that your father was not Charles?'

'I thought you were silently accusing me of deceiving you, that you would never have made even a marriage of convenience if you'd had an inkling of my true identity.'

He laughed aloud. 'It was never such a marriage, my darling, at least not on my side. I know you feel differently, but I loved you from the very start. If you had been a true dairymaid it would have made not the slightest difference. The problem lay with me. I have lost everyone I ever cared for and I couldn't bear to open my heart to the possibility of more pain.'

She tried to make sense of what he was saying. Her parentage was of no account. He loved her for who she was. And he seemed to believe that she did not love him! Her head spun as she fought through the fog of misapprehension.

'You must know I would never have hurt you,' she stammered. There was a pause as she gathered courage. 'I could not have done so – I loved you.'

He shook his head as though amazed at how blind he'd been. 'I didn't know, I didn't realise. I convinced myself otherwise. I thought you were bound to grow tired of me, perhaps play me false, or even die. One way or another I was going to lose you.'

She looked at him in astonishment.

'I know it sounds crazy but I think I *was* half-crazed. I figured that if I didn't get too close, I couldn't get hurt again.'

'And now?'

'I have been so miserable without you that I could not be more unhappy, whatever happens in the future between us.'

There was another long silence while she thought over the tangled feelings he had revealed. Then he seemed to throw caution aside, because he blurted out, 'You said a moment ago there was a time when you loved me. Do you still?'

The air appeared to hang breathless, waiting for an answer. He had hurt her and hurt her badly, but were the long days when he had left her solitary and loveless too bitter to forgive? She sat quite still, her mind floundering, unable to see her way clearly. He had laid bare his deepest emotions and she understood the conflicts that had driven him. But could she trust him sufficiently to place her life and that of their unborn child in his hands? In search of an answer she stared unseeingly into the line of trees that guarded the magical space. But they were not her salvation. She took a deep breath and looked into those dark blue eyes, and suddenly the question was no longer so difficult.

'I love you still.'

He moved a fraction towards her and she saw the longing writ plainly on his face. She put out her hand to him and he covered it with his.

'So where do we go from here?'

She heard the uncertainty and it was more than she could bear. She leaned towards him and gently touched his lips with hers. He had his arm around her and kissed her back. For several moments they sat thus, arms entwined, lips seeking solace. Then his hands were in her hair and pulling her plait to pieces.

She protested and he rolled her off the log onto the grass and swiftly followed, covering her body with his. 'The plait has to go. And so does the dress. How many times...'

'But not here,' she breathed jerkily.

'Here,' he insisted, and made short work of the grey gown.

The dress was cast aside, crumpled and slightly torn, but she hardly noticed. From now on she would wear the silks befitting her station. From now on she would be his duchess.

A chattering of birds greeted their tumble to the ground and from every corner of the glade the trees rustled their appreciation. It was as though the entire world rejoiced with them.

'We have been so long apart, I hope we have not forgot,' he murmured tenderly, divesting them both of their remaining clothes and beginning to kiss every small part of her, slowly and thoroughly.

'I think it unlikely,' she murmured back, his lips slowly rousing her to a remembered delight.

Then quite suddenly he suspended his kisses. 'What did you have to tell me?'

'Later,' she whispered, willing him not to stop.

'Why later?'

'It is a gift and you must wait.' Her precious news would be the perfect ending to a newly perfect day. 'Right now I need you to love me.'

And he did.

Other books in the Allingham Regency Classic Series:
Dance of Deception **(2017)**

About The Author

Merryn Allingham was born into an army family and spent her childhood moving around the UK and abroad. Unsurprisingly it gave her itchy feet, and in her twenties she escaped an unloved secretarial career to work as cabin crew and see the world.

The arrival of marriage, children and cats meant a more settled life in the south of England, where she's lived ever since. It also gave her the opportunity to go back to 'school' and eventually teach at university. Merryn loves the nineteenth century and grew up reading Georgette Heyer, so when she began writing herself the novels had to be Regency romances.

For more information on Merryn and her books visit http://www.merrynallingham.com/

You'll find regular news and updates on Merryn's Facebook page https://www.facebook.com/MerrynWrites/ and you can keep in touch with her on Twitter @MerrynWrites

If you enjoyed reading *Duchess of Destiny*, do please leave a review on your favourite site. Authors rely on good reviews – even just a few words – and readers depend on them to find interesting books to read.

Printed in Great Britain
by Amazon